The UNSEEN MARKET

DAVID McELROY

The Unseen Market is a work of fiction. Names, characters, places, and incidents either are the product of the author's imagination or are used factiously. Any resemblance to actual persons, living or dead, events, or locales is entirely coincidental.

ISBN-13: 978-1981169603
ISBN-10: 1981169601

Cover design: David McElroy

Illustrations: Ashleigh McElroy

First Edition

For my Viola Jane, never lose your amazing imagination.

Also by DAVID MCELROY

The Good Goblin

Contents

1. The Mad Librarian 1

2. Being Watched 9

3. A Good Afternoon for Reading 21

4. The Magician Returns.................................... 33

5. The House of Plumstone 42

6. The Hunt Begins 56

7. A Night Away 73

8. Going Somewhere 79

9. The Magician's Secret 86

10. The Old Sailor... 100

11. The Unseen Market..................................... 108

12. Empty Handed 130

13. Ghost Story 138

14. The Goblin's Secret 154

15. Ben the Human 164

16. Suspicion 170

APRIL 1902

1.
THE MAD LIBRARIAN

Not all goblins are bad. Ben, who happened to be a goblin, wished that fact was common knowledge. If it was, he probably wouldn't be running as fast as his legs could carry him through the streets and alleyways of Saint Louis right now, all the while being chased by a man shouting unfounded accusations at him.

"Thief! Thief!"

Ben, who was breathing quite heavily, had at first tried turning and shouting back, but the turning made him stray into people, buildings, and an occasional cat or dog, while the shouting just made him even more out of breath. His retaliatory diatribes seemed to fall on deaf ears anyway, so he gave up trying. Instead he focused his energy on running and holding tight onto the book in his arms.

Looking around, he realized that he no longer recognized where he was. The sound of train wheels screeching on tracks was fading further away the more he ran, so he must be either west or south of the station, the two areas he was not familiar with.

He conjured up a mental image of one of the many maps he had seen of Saint Louis. To the west led to the fairgrounds where carpenters, artisans, and laborers were busy working on plans for the next World's Fair to be held in two years' time. To the south was the Lafayette District, home to the city's nobility. The district had been largely destroyed by the great tornado of 1896 but was on the rebound and beginning to flourish once more.

As he turned a corner, he emerged into what was obviously an upper-class neighborhood with perfectly manicured lawns surrounded by wrought iron fences and playing host to some of the largest homes the goblin had yet seen in the human city.

He considered briefly jumping one of these fences and attempting to find refuge with one of the residents but a shout of "stop that goblin!" behind him quickly dashed that notion from his mind.

He was running on pure adrenaline now, and he knew if he stopped to think about his next move, he might not be able to get going again. So, he quickly made the decision to double back and make for the lighthouse. If he could reach the boat on the docks first, he stood a chance of evading his pursuer. He ran east one block and then headed back north, running as fast as he could on tired legs, while trying to pay attention to the street signs along the way. A few blocks on, he recognized the name Chouteau Avenue, which he knew ran east and west almost the entire length of the city. If he followed it east, it would take him back to the docks and from there, he might lose himself amongst the daily hustle and bustle.

He rounded the corner, grabbing hold of the street sign so as to not lose his momentum. A minute or so later, he chanced another look back and, to his dismay, found that not only was his pursuer still on his tail, but he had even gained on him slightly.

The man noticed Ben looking back at him and took the opportunity to shout at him.

"Thief! Drop that book!"

"I didn't steal it!" Ben shouted back.

The shouting had drawn even more attention to the pair and Ben could tell that more and more of the people he was passing were considering whether it was their civic duty to step in and stop this goblin thief. He needed to get off of the busy street before one of them gathered enough courage.

The good news was that he was becoming more and more familiar with his surroundings. He took a left on 12th Street, which he knew would take him to Washington Square, and from there it was less than ten blocks to the riverfront. However, no sooner had he turned the corner than he realized his mistake.

Two horse-drawn wagons had apparently crashed into each other. One was on its side and its contents, at least twenty barrels of beer, had fallen out and were rolling all directions down the street. The drivers argued, at least a dozen men were chasing the barrels, and everyone within earshot had come to witness the incident.

Ben was about to turn around but, at that moment, his pursuer rounded the corner, twenty feet away. The goblin ducked into an alley, praying to whatever gods might be listening for some bit of luck. Unfortunately, in his experience, luck tended not to favor goblins, and he ran nearly straight into a brick wall. It was a dead end.

He slumped against the wall, panting and clutching the book to his chest. The man who had been chasing him almost ran straight past the alley but stopped at the last minute and changed course.

"Ha!" he cried in triumph. "Nowhere left to run, thief!"

Ben took several deep breaths, trying to find his voice. "I told you, I didn't steal the book."

"Liar!" the man spat back at him, advancing a few steps but still keeping his distance. It was obvious that while he had no qualms about chasing a goblin, he wasn't entirely sure what to do now that he had caught one.

Ben shook his head in frustration. "I'm not lying! I didn't steal it. It's a *library* book!" he argued.

The man pointed a finger accusingly at Ben. "Of course, it is! That's how I know you stole it. *We* would never loan a book to a *goblin*."

"We?"

"I'm a librarian, you fool," the man said scathingly. "I watched you take it right out of the hands of a young woman!"

A librarian. Well, that would explain the lengths that the man had gone to recover a single book.

Ben shook his head again. "I didn't *take* it from her; she *gave* it to me! She's a friend."

The librarian stared at him for a few moments and then burst out laughing. "A friend?" he asked, nearly doubled over in laughter. "Goblins don't have *human* friends."

Ben could feel his face blushing orange and he wanted to argue back but a voice in the back of his head told him it was pointless. He took a few steps forward, which had the effect of ceasing the librarian's laughing and even made the man take a step backward.

Ben leaned down slowly and set the book on the ground. Then he went and leaned against the wall again.

"I'm not a thief," said Ben again with as much dignity as he could muster. "But apparently nothing I say will convince you of that. So, just take the book."

The librarian narrowed his eyes, as though he expected some goblin trickery. When Ben didn't move, the man edged forward slowly and picked up the book. He looked down the street in both directions, most likely to see if any policemen were patrolling nearby. Then, he seemed to make up his mind.

"Don't let me catch you anywhere near the library again," he said before turning and disappearing down the street.

2.
BEING WATCHED

Ben breathed a sigh of relief but was immediately overwhelmed with a feeling of despair. It had been three months since he had learned the truth about his father. He now knew that he wasn't the only good goblin. Ben remembered his father's words that night:

How can someone be an anomaly if another exists in his image?

Neither Ben nor his father were an anomaly — there was something more to their "condition" than either of them knew, and Ben was determined to find out what it was.

He had spent much of the time since conducting what research he could into the matter. He knew that it was a long shot, finding very specific and nigh unknown information about goblins in a human library, but it was a place to start. It had not been easy either. Since he was not allowed in the library, the task of searching had fallen to his only friend and fellow lamplighter, Maribel, who was eager to help. It had become almost a daily routine. Maribel found the books, checked them out, and then handed them over to Ben, who spent the whole of his free time that day reading until his shift on the watch began that night. The next day, she returned the book and they started all over again.

Ben had read over seventy books, which was much more than he thought a human library would carry regarding goblinkind, but so far none of them had contained even the slightest glimmer of a hint. However, this morning had been different.

"This one sounds promising," she had said when she handed it to him.

Ben glanced at the title, *Gobelin Sagas*. A twinge of remembrance prickled at the back of his mind as he read it. He scoured his memory trying to reason why it sounded so familiar, but try as he might, he couldn't recall its significance. That's when the mad librarian had burst forth from the library like a hound that had just caught the scent of a fox.

They could try again tomorrow, he thought, but it wouldn't be as easy now that the librarian would undoubtedly be on the watch for him and anyone acquainted with him. Even though Ben didn't think the man had believed him about Maribel being his friend, he might be wary of her in the future and not allow her to check that same book out again.

He was just thinking about asking Jacob to

check the book out for him when he realized he was no longer alone in the alley. He looked up and saw a tall, dark, menacing looking woman blocking his exit.

"Spare a moment for a chat?" she asked casually in an accent Ben didn't recognize.

She took a few steps closer, not in the least showing the hesitancy that the librarian had. Ben took a closer look at her. Menacing was perhaps too harsh a judgment — strong and confident may have been better adjectives. She had black hair that matched her skin and fell behind her in long curls. A scar ran down her right cheek and marred an otherwise striking face. She was dressed in an emerald cloak and wore a hat that reminded Ben of an illustration from *The Three Musketeers,* though without the fanciful plumage.

Ben tried to find his voice. "I suppose," he said tentatively.

The woman grinned. "You don't know me,"

she said, "but I know you. Do you know why that is?"

Ben shook his head, confused as to where this conversation was headed.

The woman leaned over slightly and the clasp on her cloak caught the scant sunlight that fell into the alleyway. His eyes were immediately drawn to it. It was silver and at first, he thought it was shaped like an oblong diamond, but on closer inspection, he realized that it was actually the head of a goblin with exaggeratedly long ears sticking out to form sharp points on the sides. A shiver ran through his body when he noticed that in the place of the goblin's eyes were two X's. The message was clear.

"You're a goblin hunter," he said, his voice shaking.

The woman straightened and tilted her head as if she were considering his words.

"Yyyes," she said, "and no. I am a member of

the Green Watch, which one might crudely refer to as 'goblin hunters.' However, that is not my particular, um, specialty. I find that I am quite adept at blending in to a crowd."

Ben looked at her dubiously. He couldn't imagine anyone so memorable ever truly blending in anywhere.

"I know what you're thinking," she said, and Ben blushed, hoping that weren't true. He found that he was equally terrified and fascinated by this woman.

"It's true," she continued. "I am, like you, in the minority in a city such as this. However, believe me when I say that if I don't wish to be seen, you won't see me."

Ben started to correct her that this hadn't been his line of thinking at all but decided to spare himself further embarrassment.

He nodded. "So, you do the watching for the Green Watch then?"

She smiled. "I do indeed, much like you. I

find it somewhat ironic that we have quite similar jobs. Though where you are tasked with watching over the whole of the city, my only target is *you*."

Ben felt himself shiver again at that last word. He also didn't particularly care for being labeled a "target."

"I've been watching you since the day you arrived in Saint Louis. I watched as you struggled to find a trade. I watched as you were taken away by your brother. I watched as you made a friend."

Ben's eyes widened. He wasn't sure what the result of the Green Watch's special attention to him would be, but he wouldn't be able to live with himself if he knew that he was responsible for any harm befalling Maribel.

"Leave her out of this!" he blurted out, anger rising to the surface.

The woman smiled again but some of her laid-back attitude seemed to fall away and she took a half step backward.

She regained her composure quickly though and held up her hands.

"Calm yourself. I mean no harm to you or your friend. As I said, my job is simply to watch."

Ben's heart was still racing, but he tried to calm himself down, taking long, deep breaths, knowing that losing his temper would be unwise given his present company.

"So, what exactly do you want then?" he asked, trying to control the shaking in his voice.

She looked at him for a moment without speaking. Her eyes met his, and to Ben, it felt as though she were trying to look inside him.

"I wish merely to caution you. When I first was tasked with watching you, I imagined you would be much like every other goblin I have had the displeasure of watching. You're not the first to come to a human city, and I'm being kind when I say that it usually doesn't end well."

At this, she momentarily and perhaps subconsciously reached up and felt for the clasp on her cloak.

"I expected the same from you," she continued, "but . . . you surprised me. Not only did you appear to have no ulterior motive for being here, you seemed simply to wish to blend in and be accepted.

"I was equally surprised when you managed to befriend your fellow lamplighter, to the point where she risked her life to help you. When you were taken by your brother, I knew for certain then that you weren't an ordinary goblin."

She stopped and smiled at him then, and the smile this time showed a kindness that hadn't been there before. Ben felt the blood rise to his cheeks again, and he looked away from her.

"Watching you has been merely routine since your return, until today."

He looked back up and met her eyes. There

was no accusation in them despite her words but his heartbeat began to grow more rapid once more.

"I realize that the librarian was wrong to accuse you of theft and if I felt it was my place to set it right, I would. However, I am merely a watcher and the disturbance today is one I must report to my superiors."

Ben's face fell. "But it was just a misunderstanding; you said so yourself."

The woman shook her head. "I know and I'm sorry, but there were too many people that witnessed it and I can't go to each of them and set things right. There will be complaints of a goblin causing trouble in the city and my superiors will find out regardless."

She took a step forward and leaned down again, her goblin head clasp gleaming again in the light.

"Why are you telling me all this?" Ben asked.

She considered him. "I didn't need to, but I

did because *I* know the truth and I don't wish you any ill. So, be extra careful from now on. Stay away from the library for a while. Tread lightly. My guess is that they'll want to put another watcher on you, but I'll do my best to dissuade them."

Ben nodded. "Well, thank you, I suppose."

The woman nodded and began to turn away.

"Wait," he called suddenly. She turned back to face him. "You know everything about me, but I don't even know your name."

She smiled that kind smile again. "I really shouldn't tell you this, but there is truth in your reasoning. I'm Amelia."

Ben nodded, and they appraised each other in silence for a moment more.

"Be careful, Ben. If this scene is repeated again in the near future, I'll have no other choice but to escort you out of the city."

Ben swallowed hard at that and with a final nod, Amelia turned and disappeared into a passing crowd.

3.
A Good Afternoon for Reading

Ben hurried back to the lighthouse, eager to avoid any more uncomfortable encounters. The sky had turned cloudy with the promise of oncoming rain and a cool, early spring breeze rattled the lighthouse windows. It was perfect weather for reading. He closed his door, lit the gas lamp on his bedside table, and holed up in his room for the rest of the day.

His meeting with the enigmatic Amelia had put *The Three Musketeers* into his mind, and so he pulled an old battered copy of the Dumas

21

classic off of his only bookshelf and spent the afternoon with d'Artagnan and his companions. Every once in a while, he would stop and relive the meeting with the mysterious woman before resuming his book. He was having trouble reconciling the knowledge that she had been watching him without his knowing it or even catching a glimpse at her. He knew that if he had ever seen her before, he would have remembered.

He briefly entertained the possibility that she was lying and was only trying to intimidate him. However, there had been true sincerity in her eyes when she told him he was no "ordinary goblin." Besides, aside from Maribel, Jacob, and possibly the guild master, no one else knew the particulars of his abduction last December by his brother. No other onlookers at the train station that night probably even realized that he was being abducted. All goblins tended to blend together to most human eyes. Only someone who had been watching him would know the particulars of what happened.

Ben stood and looked out of his only window. He could feel a faint coolness as air leaked through the cracks around it. Surveying the landscape, he could see no one and yet he was sure that she was out there somewhere.

Around seven o'clock, the aromas of cooked meat and spices wafted under his door. He thought about skipping dinner but knew he would be sorry for it later if he did. So, he stowed his book under his arm and made his way down to the first floor.

The whole of the floor was one large room with a fireplace opposite the front door and a line of tables from end to end. Throughout the day, the room served as a communal space for off-duty lamplighters to talk, play cards, or whatever they enjoyed doing. At seven, both a.m. and p.m., and noon, it served as the place where anyone with a hungry stomach took their meals. The kitchen was below, and no one ever really saw the cooks, but without fail, on those three hours, the tables were laden with food.

A fire crackled brightly in the hearth when Ben arrived downstairs, and he took a seat near it. He ladled some beef and vegetable stew onto a clean plate and broke off a hunk of bread. He had just taken his first bite when he felt the presence of someone sitting beside him. He turned to the red-cheeked and smiling face of his only friend, Maribel.

"What's for dinner tonight?" she asked, rubbing her hands together and blowing warm air into them.

She looked down at Ben's plate.

"Oh look, it's stew . . . again," she said, a little downcast.

"At least it's warm," Ben offered after he had swallowed.

Maribel smiled as she filled up her plate. "It

is at that," she said and then added, "Your optimism never fails to impress me."

They ate in silence for a time, Maribel thawing herself out with the warm food and Ben hungrier than he had realized.

Jacob descended the stairs and scanned the room. When he caught their eyes, he nodded briefly and then filled a plate with food and disappeared back up the stairs.

"You'd never know," said Maribel suddenly, "that there was anything more between us by the way he acts."

Ben was confused. "Between us?" he asked.

"Yeah, I mean we all went on a bit of an adventure together, didn't we? We almost *died* together. I've always heard that sort of thing is supposed to be a bonding experience, like going to war or something. From the way he acts, we might be no more than passing acquaintances."

Ben thought about this for a moment. From his viewpoint, the relationship between him and Jacob had taken a big turn for the better. Before their "so-called" adventure, Jacob had been openly hostile toward him. Ever since, they were on much friendlier terms, though he'd never call them friends. They never ate together or spent free time together or even had long conversations together, but they did acknowledge each other when they crossed paths, usually with a smile and a nod. It wasn't much, but it was an improvement.

"Oh well," Maribel's voice cut into his thoughts, "some people, I guess."

She sighed and took another bite.

"So, how's that book we checked out today?" she asked.

Ben nearly choked on the potato he was chewing. Coughing, he took a drink. When he felt comfortable speaking again, he said, "About that . . . I didn't exactly get the chance to read any of it."

He relayed the events of the morning,

starting with the crazed librarian chasing him all over the city.

Maribel's frown had deepened gradually throughout the course of his story, but she had remained silent, right up until he repeated the librarian's line about goblins not having friends. "What an ass! That's just . . . The nerve of that . . . What was he . . . Ahh!" Her cry of frustration made the two lamplighters sitting opposite them jump in their seats.

"Sorry," said Ben to the two, who were staring at Maribel questioningly.

"I'm heading straight back there tomorrow and giving that man a piece of my mind! Stealing from a young woman indeed!"

Ben was about to continue his story and tell her about Amelia, but for some reason, it caught in his throat. He told himself that he was simply sparing her more anger, for he knew that if the librarian was upsetting her this much, the knowledge that Ben had actually been spied on for the entirety of his life in Saint Louis, including all of his time spent with her, she might lose whatever small amount of composure she still possessed and do something rash.

However, the truth was that he was embarrassed. Even though he seemed to have swayed Amelia's judgment to his behalf, he couldn't help feeling like a criminal, constantly under surveillance, the Green Watch just waiting for him to slip up and give them an excuse to throw him out of their city. He was also embarrassed that someone had watched him for a year and a half and he hadn't noticed. The first few months, alright. Six months was pushing it, and a year was barely understandable, but a year and a half . . . even the thickest sort of person should have been able to notice something strange. The worst part was that any goblin in his home city of Jotunfell would have known they were being tailed from the very first night. It only served to prove how inadequate he was at even the most basic of goblin skills.

Maribel, as always, was as good as her word. The next day, she and Ben headed out for the library. Ben waited a couple blocks down the road so as not to be seen and watched as Maribel strode through the doors. Ten minutes or so later, she returned, looking as annoyed as ever.

"I'm going to guess that it didn't go well," said Ben cautiously.

Maribel shook her head and sat down on a nearby bench.

"It was going alright," she started after she had cooled down a bit. "I even had the book in my hands. Then, he said something about watching my back for goblins in the future and I sort of . . . lost my composure. I don't think they'll be letting me back in there for a while."

"Oh," said Ben. His emotions were torn. On

the one hand, here was someone who was defending him at any cost to her own reputation. That was definitely something worth being happy over. On the other hand, he was now essentially cut off from the city library, his best chance at finding answers to all of his questions.

"I'm so sorry, Ben," Maribel said, cutting into his thoughts. "I shouldn't have lost my cool like that. I just get so tired of people's prejudices. It's maddening, you know?"

Ben nodded. He definitely did know. Not a day went by when he wasn't subject to at least one comment or horrified stare.

"It's alright," he said. "Thanks for having my back. We'll just have to find another place to find books."

Maribel smiled sadly at him. "I'll think of something. Unfortunately, though, it will have to wait a little while."

"Why's that?" Ben asked.

"I just found out last night that they need me to work a different route for the next week, and it's all the way out past Forest Park. I'll probably just stay at the guild house out there during the day instead of walking all that way back every night."

The Lamplighter's Guild had locations spaced around the city, the lighthouse being just one of them. The main headquarters, where the guild master lived, was the guild house of which Maribel referred. Ben had only been there once before, but he definitely remembered it. A large three-story brick house with a steeply pitched roof and tall arched windows, completely surrounded by trees. It was technically on the grounds of the park.

"On a positive note," she continued, "at least I'll get to watch the progress on the fair. I hear they're going to build a giant wheel that people can actually ride on high into the sky!"

"I'd like to see that!" said Ben.

"We'll go together," she said, smiling.

4.
THE MAGICIAN RETURNS

Ben and Maribel spent the rest of the afternoon attempting to improve their moods. It was a sunny, warm day with no traces of the previous day's clouds. They stopped into a guild house downtown for lunch and then went to their favorite bakery near Union Station for raspberry tarts and coffee. Around half past six o'clock, when the sun was beginning to sink below the horizon, Maribel headed off toward the park and Ben made his way back to the lighthouse.

Loneliness started to creep in the moment they parted company. Not seeing her for a week was a hard thing to face. She had covered others' routes before for a day or two at a time, but never for a whole week. Ben sighed heavily and decided to just do what he had always done and bury himself in his books.

He had been looking down as he walked, not really paying much attention to his surroundings. So, when a somewhat familiar voice suddenly sounded in his ear, he nearly jumped out of his skin.

"Why the long face, kid?"

Ben looked up and immediately recognized the street magician that he had assisted the year before.

"Percival the Perplexing!" said Ben.

The magician held out his hands and chuckled. "Percival Plumstone, at your service! But please, just call me Percival, or Percy, if you wish. I had an aunt called me that. Lovely lady."

Ben nodded, extending his hand. "Ben Tam . . ." He stopped abruptly before he could finish. He wasn't sure what unconscious force had held his tongue, but he found that he agreed with it. Everyone in this city knew of his father. If he was to better ingratiate himself here, it might be best to not admit to being the son of a feared goblin leader.

"Ben Tamm," he said again, more confidently.

"Are you sure?" asked Plumstone with a wry smile.

"Definitely," said Ben with an air of confidence.

"Ben Tamm it is then! A pleasure to once again make your acquaintance," he said, shaking the goblin's hand heartily.

They walked a few more steps together and Plumstone's face changed slightly.

"I don't wish to alarm you," he said in a much

quieter tone, "but the true reason that I sought you out just now is because I noticed something."

Ben felt panic start to rise in him, and he looked around nervously. "What is it?" he asked.

"Well, I believe you are being followed," said Plumstone, an air of worry evident in his voice.

Ben felt the panic subside. "Green cloak?" he asked.

"Yes indeed." Plumstone frowned and nodded. "But how did you . . ."

"We sort of ran into each other yesterday. Apparently, she's been following me since I first arrived in town."

Plumstone's frown deepened. "Truly? And she told you this?"

Ben nodded. "It was more of a friendly warning. She's with the Green Watch."

He stopped and turned around quickly, hoping to catch her off-guard. He focused his eyes, surveying the scene behind him, a busy street at dusk. People were scrambling about, finishing up their shopping for the day. He searched everywhere but couldn't see any trace of Amelia.

He shrugged and began walking again.

Plumstone still looked concerned. "You seem strangely alright with this," he said.

"What choice do I have?" Ben asked. "She wouldn't stop following me even if I asked her to. I'm a goblin in a human city. They're just being careful."

"Yes, but surely it would take no longer than a day at most to determine whether you are threat to the city or its people. I can tell that, and I've known you for less than fifteen minutes."

Plumstone walked for a moment in silence before stating, "You know, I could do something about this. I am a magician, after all."

"Are you going to make plums grow on me, too, and pass me off as a tree?" Ben couldn't help smiling at the thought.

Plumstone frowned. "I can do more than make fruit grow, you know."

Ben nodded. "Happen to know any tricks that could get me into the library?" he asked, his thoughts once more drifting to the book.

"The library?" asked Plumstone, his forehead creasing in confusion.

Ben hesitated for a moment. He had been about to mention his research, but doing so would reveal his father's secret — the one his father had sacrificed his life's happiness to keep.

"I love to read," he stated truthfully. While Ben thought he could trust the magician, it was true that he had only known him for a short span of time. But he did like Plumstone well enough and didn't want to lie to him.

"Truly? I've heard that about goblins," said

Plumstone, "though I don't think you'll find too many goblin classics in any library around here."

"Actually," said Ben, "I'm not too interested in those. I read most of them as a child. My favorites are stories written by humans."

"Is that so?" Plumstone smiled. "I suppose I shouldn't be surprised given everything else I know about you, but it does come as a bit of a shock. From what I know of goblins, they would very much look down on such a habit."

Ben nodded in agreement. "Oh, they do. That's why I'm here, well, partly why I'm here."

After a few moments of silence, Ben realized that the magician was no longer walking alongside him, and he stopped to see where his companion had gone.

"Is something wrong?" he asked, turning around.

Plumstone stood ten feet or so behind him with an introspective look on his face, watching

Ben.

Ben wondered what Plumstone saw. He knew he looked out of place against the backdrop of the city: a small green form walking as casually as could be while all of the light- and dark-skinned humans passed him by, giving him a little bit wider of a berth than was necessary. Yet if they only gave him the chance, they'd find him more akin to themselves than they ever would have thought possible.

Plumstone visibly shook off his thoughts and approached the goblin, smiling. "I think I may be able to help you," he said.

"Really?"

"Though I can't get you into the library, per se, I can get you access to enough books to last you for some time. Are you interested?"

Ben couldn't help but smile at that, and he nodded his head vigorously. The magician reached into one of his coat pockets and produced a card, which he handed over.

Ben took it and quickly glanced at its contents. It read "Percival Ronald Plumstone, Master Magician." He turned it over to see a street address.

"Come to this address in the morning and I'll tell you more."

5.
THE HOUSE OF PLUMSTONE

It was a lucky thing for the citizens of Saint Louis that no trouble descended upon them that night, for the first watcher who would spot such trouble was more distracted than he let on.

Ben spent the whole of his watch walking in circles around the lighthouse's circumference, not searching for potential dangers but merely attempting to catch even the briefest of glimpses of Amelia.

However, no matter how long or hard he looked, his expert goblin eyesight couldn't catch a glimpse of anyone matching the image in his head of the dark lady of the Green Watch. Perhaps it hadn't been her skin at all that had been dark, he mused to himself. Perhaps she was just made up entirely of shadow and could only be seen when she wished it.

That next morning, after he had managed a few hours of sleep, he sprang out of bed, eager to be on his way to meet the magician. Plumstone hadn't specified an exact time, but he had mentioned morning, so Ben didn't want to take the chance that he'd be late.

He opened his window and stuck his head outside. The night's spring chill was in the process of warming over and the cloudless sky promised another day much like the last.

Around ten o'clock, Ben stopped in front of a house at the corner of Mississippi and Lafayette Avenue. The magician was waiting outside for him, wearing a top hat of a violent shade of pink.

"Welcome to my home," said Plumstone, gesturing to the house proudly. "I wore the hat so you wouldn't overlook me!"

Ben was momentarily speechless. The house was one of the most beautiful that the goblin had ever seen. It was constructed primarily of red brick with arched windows and an arched green front door. The main part of the house was two stories with a curved mansard-style roof covered in multi-colored diamond-shaped shingles. On its west side was a three-story tower with a large circular window on the top floor and a roof that matched the rest of the house. It was not the largest house that Ben had seen in Saint Louis, but all the same, to say that it was impressive was underselling it by a long shot.

"It's . . . wow," said Ben.

Plumstone grinned. "I would have to agree," he said. "Oddly enough, it was originally built to be a police headquarters."

The magician put his hand on Ben's shoulder and motioned him to the front door.

"So, how did you come by owning it?"

Plumstone shrugged. "I . . . know people . . . who know people," he stammered slowly and then quickly added, "I'm sure it's all rather uninteresting to you. The bottom line is I was able to acquire it two years prior and do not foresee letting it go anytime soon."

They were three or four paces away from the front door when it opened and a young lady Ben recognized appeared behind it. When he had last seen her, he had taken her for a girl of only eleven years but now that he saw her again, he realized that she was more likely several years older than that, probably only a few years younger than he was.

She had dark black hair, slightly pale skin, and piercing blue eyes. In contrast to the colorful clothing of her companion, she wore a modest dark blue dress with white lace detailing on the sleeves and neckline. She smiled as she held the door open to him.

"Miss . . . Clara, I believe?"

The young lady blushed and nodded. "Quite right. I'm surprised you remembered," she said sweetly.

Ben felt his own face begin to blush, and he quickly blurted out, "I read a lot, so I have a pretty decent head for names."

Clara nodded and opened the door wider, stepping to the side. "Won't you come in?"

Ben entered the great house, followed by a smirking Plumstone.

"Clara, my dear, as I was telling you last night, this is Ben Tamm. I can see you remember each other."

Ben and Clara both realized they were still staring at each other, and in unison, turned their gazes elsewhere.

Collecting herself, Clara asked politely, "Might I interest you in a cup of tea or coffee?"

"Coffee, please, if it's not too much trouble," said Ben.

"No trouble at all. Can I take your coat and hat?" She held out her arms and Ben handed over his affects.

Clara smiled and disappeared through a nearby doorway.

Ben took a quick moment to look around. The interior was just as majestic as the exterior, though not nearly as tidy. This, Ben would soon realize, was solely the magician's doing. His eccentricities did not stop with his clothes and he seemed to leave a constant stream of messes in his wake. Clara, for her part, was exactly the opposite, and by the end of the first day that he spent at the house of Plumstone, he could see that she spent most of her time undoing her mentor's untidinesses.

"This way, my friend," said Plumstone after he had removed his hat and tossed it haphazardly onto a pile of books, which had clearly been removed from a nearby shelf and stacked in a loose pile quite recently.

Ben followed, and the magician led him down a hallway, up two flights of stairs, and into a square-shaped room that could only be the top of the tower he had glimpsed from the street.

Outside of humorous illustrations, the term "jaw-dropping" is not a truly accurate description of a real living being's reaction upon seeing something that greatly surprises or excites them, no matter if they're human or goblin. "Jaw-slightly-opening" might be a better term. However, I can assure you that if ever a jaw did drop in the history of our world, it was on this day and it was the jaw of a good goblin named Ben.

The room was tall, that was the first thing he noticed. The very close second thing he noticed were the sheer number of books that lined the walls. In a normal study, one might have shelves that make up the majority of one, two, or maybe even three walls. These shelves typically leave room for other decorations and most usually a grand, cozy fireplace. The magician's library, on the contrary, had shelves covering every possible square inch of space in the room, save for the four circular windows that looked out on each of the four walls, and every bit of space on those shelves was inhabited by books.

"You have no fireplace," Ben thought out loud, his brain still processing the magnificence of this sight.

Plumstone smirked. "I would like to know what fool first thought that it was a good idea to put a fireplace in a study," he stated bluntly. "A large open flame sitting directly in the midst of stacks of nice dry paper. In my eyes, no man or woman who truly loves books will ever be found with a fireplace in their library."

Ben was slightly taken aback. "Well . . . it

does make for comfortable reading, you can't argue that."

"True," the magician conceded. "That's why I have a separate reading room, which I shall show you later."

Ben turned his attention back to the books but did not move. Plumstone looked at him bemused for a while before finally saying, "You can touch them, you know."

Ben smiled broadly but said nothing. Plumstone laughed out loud.

"It's obviously not as expansive of a selection as the illustrious Saint Louis Public Library, but I thought it might provide a decent diversion for a while."

Ben took a slow step forward and then like a child in a sweets store, he fell upon the books eagerly, his eyes taking in their titles as quickly as he could read. A few months ago, he would have been content to just take the first book he saw, read through it, and then move on to the next. Now, he had only one book in mind.

He made his way around the room, scouring the shelves he could reach, before ascending to the narrow catwalk that wrapped around the upper echelons of the bookshelves.

An hour or so later, Clara entered the room with a tray bearing a pot of tea, two empty mugs, a cup of coffee, and a plate of shortbread cookies. She set them down on the desk and Plumstone followed, eagerly eyeing the cookies.

"I apologize for taking so long," she said, "but we didn't have any cookies, muffins, or, well, anything fitting for company. The only ingredients I had were for these, so I hope you like them."

Ben descended the stairs and joined, looking a little dejected.

"You don't like shortbread?" asked Plumstone.

Ben shook his head, not realizing he was

wearing his emotions so visibly. "Oh no, it's not that. I do quite like shortbread, well, at least I think I do. I've only smelled them when passing by the bakery. I should most like to try them."

Clara blushed and handed the goblin his coffee and a cookie.

"So, why the long face?" asked Plumstone, settling himself into a chair and motioning for Ben to do the same.

Ben took a bite of the cookie. It tasted even better than he had imagined.

"These are delicious," he said. "Thank you."

Behind her cup of tea, Clara smiled.

"You don't happen to own a copy of *Gobelin Sagas*, do you?" Ben asked after he had finished his first cookie.

Plumstone thought for a moment and then shook his head. "No, I can't say that do. I take it that's what you've been searching for?"

Ben nodded. "The public library has it, but they won't allow me to check out books there."

Clara frowned. "Why not?" she asked.

"He's a goblin," stated Plumstone bluntly before Ben could reply.

"Oh right," said Clara.

"My question is," said Plumstone, "how do you know they have it if you're not allowed in?"

Ben hesitated for a moment, trying to decide whether he was breaking Maribel's trust by telling others about her role in sneaking library books to him. Ultimately, he realized that he trusted his new acquaintances and somehow knew they wouldn't give her away.

"My friend Maribel, she . . . helped me for a while. She would check out books and then give them to me."

"That was very kind of her," Plumstone said. "I would venture to guess that it didn't end well?"

Ben nodded.

"A couple days ago actually. One of the librarians saw her give a book to me and assumed I'd stolen it," he said. "He took great pains in retrieving it."

Plumstone's eyebrows raised as dawning comprehension flooded his face. "Ah, so the rumor is true. I heard tell of a man chasing a goblin through the streets. I presume said goblin was you?"

Ben nodded again.

Plumstone sighed heavily. "Quite the extent to go to in order to retrieve a single book."

"I thought so," said Ben, feeling the soreness in his legs, which had really begun to creep up on him that morning.

"And the book? It was this *Myths and Folklore of Goblins*?" asked Plumstone.

"It was," Ben confirmed. "I hadn't even had a chance to open it yet."

"Why do you want it so bad then if you hadn't even read it?" asked Clara. Her tone of voice was innocently curious.

Blushing, Ben thought once again about how

much he should divulge. Before he had made up his mind, though, Plumstone interjected.

"If you don't wish to tell us, that is your business and we shall not pry any further. Unfortunately, my friend, while I have heard of the book, I do not possess it. Perhaps Clara or I could attempt to retrieve it from the library for you?"

Excitement began to flood through Ben, the same excitement that he had felt when he first saw the book. Before he could even thank them, though, Clara jumped up, spilling the small amount of tea left in her cup.

"I'll go!" she said enthusiastically. Without waiting for a reply, she rushed out the door, leaving the spilled cup and puddle of tea on the floor behind her.

"I suppose that settles that," Plumstone said, smirking. "Another cookie while we wait?"

6.
The Hunt Begins

Clara returned as the sun was beginning its descent beyond the horizon. The setting star shone directly through the library's west window, casting a circle of light on the opposing wall. Ben had spent the time waiting engaged in The House of the Seven Gables, which had come to his mind when he first saw the magician's house earlier that day.

The look on Clara's face and the absence of a book in her arms told Ben all he needed to know.

"I had the book in my hands," she said, slumping back into the chair she had vacated hours before. "When I went to check it out, though, the librarian told me that the book had been marked 'restricted.'"

Ben frowned. "What does that mean?"

"It means that you can only read it *in* the library. It's not allowed off of the premises," she explained.

Plumstone whistled. "You must have really upset that librarian."

Ben sighed. "Yeah, I suppose so," he said resignedly. "Well, I guess I'll try some of the bookshops in the city."

"You should try the one on Market Street first," offered Plumstone. "I've found plenty of good tomes there and it's on your way back home in any case."

Clara shook her head. "I already tried there," she said, then added, "That's what took me so long. It really is a massive shop."

They all sat in silence for a while until Plumstone stood up abruptly and declared, "We need food! I'm sure full stomachs will help us think clearer on this matter."

Ben was about to agree, as he had not eaten a bite since the cookies, but a glance at the clock forced him to change his mind.

"I wish I could, but if I don't head back now, I won't make it in time for my watch."

"A raincheck then," said Plumstone. "Lunch, tomorrow? Perhaps after, we might stop in to a few literary establishments I know of."

"Of course, but . . . you're going to help me look for the book? Why?"

Plumstone shrugged. "Let's just say you've piqued my curiosity and besides, we outcasts must stick together!"

Ben frowned, but not because he minded being referred to as an outcast. "Outcast? But you're a human."

Plumstone smiled a wry smile. "True, but I

don't exactly blend in to the crowd, if you catch my meaning. Never have."

Ben nodded his understanding, though he wasn't sure he agreed. Still, he appreciated the gesture of camaraderie and gladly accepted it. "Tomorrow then?" he asked.

"Tomorrow," agreed Plumstone.

"Goodnight, Miss Clara," Ben said, tipping his cap politely.

The girl blushed. "Just Clara is fine and goodnight to you."

* * *

The next day at noon, Ben returned to the house in the park and found a feast of sliced ham, diced potatoes, biscuits, green corn, and cabbage salad, alongside large glasses of freshly squeezed lemonade already laid out on the dining room table.

The dining room was not overly large but still elegant. It was the only room in the house that appeared to be in a small semblance of order and thus, Ben rightly assumed that it did not get much regular use. In one corner was a decorative fireplace, and in the other, a phonograph with a large brass horn caught the sunlight, which shined through the windows and reflected through the many crystals dangling from the ornate chandelier.

Ben had heard of phonographs before but had never seen one in action. Plumstone carefully selected a record, placed it on the turntable, and wound the crank. A slow, relaxing jazz beat crackled to life through the horn and filled the room with its ambiance.

Ben took a seat at the table, and for a while they simply exchanged pleasantries with no mention of restricted books, libraries, or goblin hunters. For a few precious moments, Ben allowed himself to forget his troubles and simply enjoy the camaraderie and peace that had unexpectedly entered his life.

Camaraderie was precisely what it felt like,

too. He couldn't quite put his finger on it, but there was something different about this new burgeoning friendship with the magician and his apprentice from the one he shared with Maribel. Without a doubt, Maribel was practically the greatest friend anyone could wish for. She had befriended him when the rest of the world wouldn't give him a chance and had sacrificed her own safety to help him. However, when he spoke to Percival and Clara, there was something in the words, the things that they spoke about, that felt different. Perhaps it was simply their more advanced knowledge of goblinkind and their customs. There was an instant familiarity there, an understanding of his background that Maribel was only just beginning to fully grasp.

Ben noticed with a half-hidden smirk that Plumstone had cleaned his plate by the time Ben was only halfway through his. Plumstone didn't appear impatient, though, and he spent the remaining time that it took Clara and Ben to finish regaling them with stories of where and how he had acquired the various paintings hanging on the walls around them. Ben particularly enjoyed the story about the cobbler and the painting of the peach pie.

When at last their appetites were satisfied, they all put on their coats, hats, and scarves.

"By my counting," said Plumstone, locking the front door behind them, "there are eleven bookshops in the city. With any luck, we can search them all by nightfall!"

He hailed a cab, and they all climbed inside. The driver looked curiously at Ben but a handful of coins from Plumstone made any protestations die in his throat.

"The hunt begins!" declared Plumstone enthusiastically as their carriage pulled away.

While he had counted accurately in regard to the number of bookshops in the city, the magician's estimation of time was slightly off.

They did not complete their search by nightfall of that day, nor by nightfall of the next day. It was only in the late afternoon of the third day that they at last had completed their long and, unfortunately, fruitless hunt.

When they returned to the magician's home on the last day, they adjourned to the drawing room with fresh cups of coffee in their hands. The room itself was much the same as the study, only a little tidier and with less books. Ben and Clara sat down in two plush wingback chairs that stood on opposite sides of the hearth. Plumstone tossed a few logs onto the cool ashes and began to stoke a fresh fire. A rack of pipes took center stage on the mantle and a violin hung on the wall behind it. The magician plucked up the top pipe and, borrowing a lit stick from the fire, puffed at it until it too caught. A satisfied sigh blew from his lips. Then he took up the violin and, without explanation, began to run the bow over the strings.

Suffice it to say, Percival Plumstone was not an accomplished violinist. In fact, if Ben had to guess, he would have probably ventured that the magician was playing the instrument for the first time in his life.

After a couple minutes of screeching out some notes, if one could even call them notes, Plumstone stopped and set the violin back on top of the mantle. Clara, who had seemed unaffected by the horrendous sound, reached up under her hair and pulled out two pieces of wax that she must have slipped in when Ben wasn't looking.

"Sorry," she said to Ben, a guilty look on her face. "I should have warned you. It's his newest obsession."

"It's just not working yet," said Plumstone to no one in particular.

Ben turned his attention to the magician. "Sorry, what's not working?"

"The violin. I bought it to help me think. Always seems to work wonders for Holmes when he needs to concentrate. I thought it might do the same for me."

"Perhaps it works for him because he actually knows how to play it," said Clara moodily, voicing Ben's precise thoughts. It was clear she and Percival had had this conversation before. "Plus, there's always the part about him being a fictional character, too," she added cheekily.

Ben could see the magician preparing to launch a retort, so he quickly blurted out, "Thank you for all of your help."

The words died in Plumstone's throat and he instead took a long drag on his pipe. "Right, sorry," he said after blowing out the smoke. "Not much help, though, in the end."

It was clear that the unsuccessful book hunting had put everyone in a bit of a downcast mood.

"Not at all!" interjected Ben. "Without you, it would have taken me ages to search through all of those shops by myself! Some of them might not have even let me inside. If nothing else, you've saved me time."

Plumstone's face lightened a bit, and a new fire seemed to light within him. He began to pace in front of the fire while Clara and Ben watched.

"You're right, we mustn't get discouraged," he said finally. "We simply must review the facts and decide the next steps."

He puffed on his pipe a little more and then cleared his throat. It was more than obvious that, of the three of them, the magician was used to being the center of attention and, in fact, thrived on it.

"Right, now, let's see. There is only one copy of this book in the whole city, as far as we know. No bookshops carry it, which makes it highly unlikely that any shop in any of the surrounding villages or towns would carry it also. The aforementioned *only* copy is located in the Saint Louis Public Library but can only be accessed upon gaining entry to said library, which unfortunately does not allow entry to goblins. Does that about sum it up?"

Clara and Ben both nodded. Plumstone stopped pacing, took another long puff on his pipe, and crossed his arms.

"Very well, then as I see it, we have two options. The first, we find someplace else that might sell it. The second, we figure out a way to disguise Ben so that he may enter the library and read the book at his leisure. Fortunately for us, both of these options can be potentially completed in the same place."

Ben's eyes widened in surprise. "And what place is that?" he asked.

Plumstone smiled slyly but said nothing. Instead, he dashed to the door and slammed it shut before drawing all of the curtains.

He returned to Ben's side and leaned in close.

"The Unseen Market," he said in a voice so low it was practically a whisper.

Silence filled the room as the words lingered in the air like a dense cloud of smoke. Ben had never heard of an Unseen Market, but the name alone held enough mystery to set his curiosity in motion.

"How soon is the next one?" asked Clara in a voice equally as soft.

"Hmm . . ." Plumstone stood back up and began to wave his pipe through the air as he wordlessly worked out the calculations in his head.

"Let's see," he murmured. "Every other new moon . . . after the winter solstice . . . the last was February the Eighth . . . making the next new moon . . ."

"Tuesday," said Clara, finishing the magician's thoughts.

"Precisely! Meaning that we have but two days to prepare! Not as much time as I would have liked, however, it is most fortuitous that we didn't miss it entirely, else we'd be waiting until June!"

Plumstone was suddenly a flurry of motion as he crossed the room back and forth, grabbing at objects and either tucking them under an arm or tossing them nonchalantly to Clara.

"Much to do, much to do," he repeated in a low voice while he moved.

Ben wanted to interject but he was afraid to break the magician's concentration, and it wasn't until both Plumstone and Clara, their arms fit to bursting, were about to walk out of the room, when he finally cleared his throat.

"Excuse me."

Plumstone and Clara both jumped in surprise, as though they had forgotten there was anyone else there. They both turned to

Ben.

"I'm sorry to interrupt but . . . what exactly *is* the Unseen Market?"

"Shhh!" Plumstone and Clara hushed in unison.

"Sorry."

Plumstone carefully set everything he was holding and sat down in the chair next to Ben. "Not here, not now. We mustn't speak of it with so many ears around."

Ben looked around but the only ears he knew of in the room were the magician's, Clara's, and his own.

"We'll explain on the way," said Plumstone.

"On the way?" asked Ben.

"To the market, of course. It's not here in the city. We'll have to travel a short distance to reach it."

"You mean I can come?" asked Ben, excitement building inside of him despite the fact that he still had no idea what an Unseen

Market actually was.

"Of course! That is, if you want to."

Ben nodded enthusiastically. "Oh, I do! How long will it take to get there?"

Plumstone took another puff on his pipe. "Oh, roughly five to seven hours, depending on how far the carriage is traveling that day. If they're only going as far as Dickens, where we'll stop off, the driver might push his horses a bit harder and we'll make better time. On the other hand, if it's headed as far as Springfield . . ."

He finished his sentence with a shrug and Ben was satisfied with the answer. However, a new thought had just entered his mind. If the Unseen Market was held at night, he would have to miss a night of his watch, something he had only done when he'd been abducted by his brother.

He knew that it wasn't unheard of to get a night off, however, he would need to get the permission of one of his superiors, namely Jacob. Looking at the clock hanging over the fireplace, Ben panicked when he saw the time, nearly a quarter to seven already, which only gave him an hour to get back before his shift started. He could hardly expect to be given a night off if he was late tonight.

"Thank you both again for all of your help the past few days, and for allowing me to come to the," he dropped his voice to a whisper, "market with you."

Plumstone patted Ben on the shoulder. "It's no trouble at all," he said. "We were probably going regardless, and we're happy for your continued companionship."

"I second that," said Clara from across the room. "It gets tedious only having him for company all the time!"

7.
A Night Away

Getting permission from Jacob didn't prove to be quite as difficult as Ben had imagined. He had made it back to the lighthouse and ascended the spiraling stairs to the top with a few minutes to spare. When his shift ended the next morning, he went straight to Jacob's room and knocked softly on the door.

"Yes?" came a voice from the other side.

Ben hesitated, not sure whether he should open the door and enter or simply shout his request through the door. He hadn't actually been invited in.

Several quiet seconds passed before Ben heard footsteps and Jacob calling again, this time in a harsher tone.

"What is it? I don't have time to waste on foolish pranks. If I find . . ."

His voice faltered as he swung the door open and saw Ben standing outside with an awkward grin on his face.

"Oh, it's you," said Jacob, his voice returning to a normal tone. "Why didn't you just come in?"

Ben hesitated. "I'm sorry, I didn't know if I should wait to be invited."

Jacob shook his head and stepped aside, motioning the goblin inside. "Please come in," he said politely.

Ben shuffled inside, and Jacob closed the door behind him. He returned to his desk and motioned Ben to take a seat opposite.

Though neither of them spoke of it, they

both remembered the last time they had been in these same positions: Jacob sitting behind his desk, Ben opposite. Though Ben didn't know it, Jacob looked back on the incident with a bit of shame in his heart at how he had behaved that day. Ben simply was glad that this time he didn't fear Jacob was about to sack him.

"What can I help you with?" asked Jacob, breaking both of their reveries.

Ben took a moment to recollect his thoughts.

"I was wondering, well, that is to say, I was hoping that . . . well, I would like to, um, request a night a . . . away," he stammered. He could feel his cheeks burning with embarrassment and the confused look on Jacob's face while he had listened patiently only served to make Ben more embarrassed.

Jacob rubbed his head. "Are you asking for time off from your watch?"

Ben nodded, a little too enthusiastically.

Jacob's brow furrowed a bit. "Which

night?"

"Tuesday, that is, tomorrow night."

With Maribel being away for the week, Ben knew Jacob was already down one lamplighter and the man who had just relieved Ben would be working double the time today, all morning and all afternoon, so it wasn't fair to ask him to then work tomorrow night as well. Ben waited nervously as Jacob regarded him in silence for what seemed like forever.

The truth was that it wasn't a convenient time for Ben to take a night away, however, Jacob still felt as though he owed Ben some recompense, both for the fact that he had been partly responsible for Ben's abduction and because Ben's father had saved his life.

At last he sighed and nodded. "That would be fine," said Jacob.

Ben beamed, and his nervousness fell away. "Thank you!" he said. "I really appreciate this Jacob, thank you!"

Jacob returned his smile. "Do you have plans in mind or do you just need the time away?" he asked conversationally.

"Oh, I have plans," Ben started and then hesitated briefly. Plumstone wouldn't want anyone else knowing his secret, and the Unseen Market wasn't exactly common knowledge. "I'm going on a short trip with some friends," he finished.

Ben wasn't entirely sure, but for a moment, Jacob's brow seemed to furrow ever so slightly and he thought he detected an edge to Jacob's voice when he asked, "Friends? Would that include Maribel?"

"Oh no, Maribel is in the Park District this week," Ben said. "It's some other friends. I doubt you know them."

"Right, of course," Jacob replied, his face reddening. "Well, I have much work to be getting on with, so, if you don't mind . . ."

Ben stood immediately. "Oh right, yes,

sorry. Don't let me keep you and thank you again!"

"You're welcome," said Jacob.

Ben closed the door behind him and breathed a sigh of relief. Though he couldn't see it, Jacob did the same.

8.
GOING SOMEWHERE

The moment his watch ended on Tuesday morning, Ben raced down the stairs to the main floor of the lighthouse, stopping only to grab a small satchel he had packed the night before. A small two-man rowboat sat waiting for him outside. He untied its mooring, jumped in, and rowed as fast as his tired arms could manage toward the city docks.

Plumstone and Clara were waiting for him when he arrived, his arms burning and his forehead covered in a fresh coat of perspiration.

It was still early morning and the streets were not yet busy. A light fog hovered over the docks and the dark clouds overhead warned of a coming storm.

Ben tied up the boat, hefted his bag onto his shoulder, and went to join his new friends. Plumstone stepped forward and offered to take his satchel from him, which Ben gladly obliged. Clara fell into step beside him.

"Long night?" she asked.

"Same as any other," Ben said, shrugging. "Nice and quiet. Why do you ask?"

"You just look tired is all. I would be, too, if I had stayed up all night long."

"He can sleep on the way," said Plumstone, hefting the satchel up on to the back of a waiting carriage. Several other bags and suitcases were already in place, and the magician took a short while rearranging them so that they all fit neatly. Then he opened the door and motioned for Ben and Clara to enter.

As Ben took his first step up, the sound of boots on cobblestone and a low whistle behind him drew his attention. He turned to see none other than Amelia standing ten paces or so away. Her arms were crossed, and she had a questioning look on her face.

"Going somewhere?" she asked. Her voice was not angry, simply curious.

Ben started to explain but Plumstone interjected.

"Percival Plumstone, my lady. You must be Amelia," he said, closing the distance between him and Amelia shockingly fast. He reached for her hand, but she refused to budge and glared at the colorfully dressed magician with the fancy manners. Undeterred, he continued.

"We, my apprentice and I, are taking the boy on a little excursion into the countryside. To the town of Dickens, to be more precise."

Amelia looked dubious. "I see, and what exactly are you planning on doing in Dickens,

Mr. Plumstone?"

Plumstone shrugged. "Culture."

"Culture? In Dickens?"

"Culture does not need a large population to exist. It can be found in the largest cities or the smallest villages," explained Plumstone. "You only need to know how to look."

Amelia didn't look convinced, but she sighed resignedly. "Well, I'm not sure about all that, but if I had to venture a guess, I would say it is probably something to do with all of those bookshops you've been visiting over the past few days. I take it you didn't find what you were looking for."

Ben blushed, and Clara looked ready to protest, but Plumstone once again spoke first.

"You've a keen mind, my lady. It's clear you are well placed in your profession. I do happen to know of a shop or two where I think we may have some more luck."

The crease on her brow softened a bit.

"Right, well. I suppose that's harmless enough."

She stopped talking and seemed to be thinking on the matter. Plumstone remained silent at that point. Finally, she stepped past the magician and approached Ben.

"Very well, you have my leave to go. My jurisdiction only lasts as far as the river. I could assign a new member of the Watch to take my place but, considering you'll be in the presence of two humans of some social standing," Plumstone scoffed silently behind her, which he tried and failed to turn into a throat clearing cough, "I suppose that won't be necessary. I'm going to trust you, Ben."

She nodded at him and Ben returned the gesture, though as she turned to leave, he couldn't help but notice the early sun's light reflecting off of the goblin head clasp on her green cloak. He repressed a shudder.

"You," she said, pointing to Plumstone. "If anything goes south, I'm holding you responsible."

Plumstone smiled a bit nervously and Ben realized this was the first time he had seen anyone disarm the magician's calm, confident manner so.

"Have no fear, my lady. He's in good hands with us. We'll be back within a day. You'll barely notice we're gone."

Amelia didn't respond but nodded curtly and disappeared in the dawn shadows stretching over the docks.

Plumstone turned back to Ben and sighed heavily.

"I like her!" declared Clara as she turned to climb into the carriage. "I mean, despite the fact that she's spying on you and all," she added to Ben.

The carriage was larger than most, with a bench on both sides of the doors. It was drawn by two horses, one white with black spots and one black with white spots. A driver sat on the bench behind them and Ben assumed he had already been paid handsomely because he kept his eyes straight ahead and seemed not to care about the goblin getting ready to climb into his carriage.

Ben and Clara sat on one side and Plumstone on the other. When they had all situated themselves, the magician tapped the window behind him and the driver snapped the reigns. They were off.

9.
THE MAGICIAN'S SECRET

"I believe the pace we are setting now is loud enough to drown out any eavesdroppers," Plumstone said.

It took every bit of willpower Ben possessed to tear his eyes away from the scenery when Plumstone began to speak. Ben couldn't help but feel excitement at being on the open road. His only other carriage rides had been as they searched the city's bookshops and during his escape from Jotunfell when he'd been stowed away in the back of a wagon. But this was an altogether different experience.

Glancing quickly to the driver, Plumstone continued. "You were asking about exact nature of the Unseen Market."

Ben nodded, trying to curtail his enthusiasm at everything that was happening to him at that moment. Going on a journey with new friends, riding in a proper carriage, not hidden away, and heading to a mysterious market that could only be spoken about in hushed tones. It was very hard for him to keep his excitement contained to a respectable level.

"Hmm, where to begin ... the Unseen Market, well, I suppose in the simplest terms, is a market like any other in nature. However, this particular market is for, um, *certain* clientele only. Not the usual, everyday ho-hum clientele, mind. People like, well, like me, I suppose."

Ben frowned; he wasn't really sure what the magician was getting at. "Uniquely dressed?" Ben ventured a guess.

Plumstone's grin widened across his face. "I am that indeed, though I was more referring to *what* I do."

"So, it's a market for performers?"

Plumstone's grin faltered. "Performers? Well, yes, I am that, too. Though, in actuality, I was referring to . . ."

"He's a magician; he does magic. The people at the market do magic," said Clara impatiently.

The other two looked at her and then Ben cracked a hesitant smile.

Throughout the course of his literary exploits, Ben had discovered that humans seemed to be obsessed with the idea of magic. Whether it was Merlin from *Le Morte d'Arthur*, Circe from *The Odyssey*, or Prospero from *The Tempest*, the idea of and the ability to do magic had always fascinated and frightened humans. However, to his knowledge, no human could actually *do* magic.

"Magic? Humans can't do magic," he said

through his grin. When he noticed that neither Plumstone nor Clara were smiling, he added, "Can they?"

"*Some* humans can," Plumstone said hesitantly.

Ben thought back to the first time he had met the magician, during one of his street performances. The plum tree that Ben had been tasked with holding had seemingly grown from a seed to a fruit-bearing tree in a matter of seconds, but he had just supposed it to be a trick.

"It was just a trick, right?" he said, echoing his thoughts.

Plumstone smiled a crooked smile. "My friend, prepare to be amazed by Percival the Perplexing."

❊ ❊ ❊

Though it wasn't the most ideal of locales for a display of magic, Ben watched over the next twenty or so minutes, as Plumstone performed a series of "tricks" aimed at convincing him that the magician was indeed a magically-inclined human.

The first few "tricks" began to sway Ben's convictions but once Plumstone re-performed the plum tree illusion, this time without a cloth covering the tree, he was convinced.

"How is this possible?" asked Ben, wondering at the source of such unknown power.

Visibly exhausted from the efforts of producing magic, Plumstone lowered his arms. "There are things in this world not found in books . . . at least not in the books one might come across in a library. A very small number of humans are born with these abilities and they . . . we maintain a close-knit, well-hidden community. The Unseen Market is only held under the new moon to lessen the chances of discovery."

"So, why do your magic on the street for all

to see?"

"I believe you already know the answer to that question, my friend. Did you believe that I was performing *real* magic when you watched me?"

Ben thought for a moment, but he did, in fact, already know the answer. He shook his head slowly. "No, I suppose I didn't."

"Of course, you didn't, and it is worth noting that I received over fifty dollars that night in generous tips."

"So, you do it to make money?"

"Do you really think that I could afford all that I have," Plumstone held up his arms, gesturing grandly, "working as a lamplighter or really any other profession not inherited through my family?"

"Probably not."

"Definitely not. I have expensive tastes, bountiful needs, and no family connections. There's no way that I could live as I live *and* continue my research unabated without the money that I make from using my, um, talents."

Ben frowned. "Isn't that a bit . . . dishonest," he said meekly.

Plumstone's eyebrows rose. He was about to say something but closed his mouth. Then, he, too, frowned. "I suppose it is, in a way. Though, people give me money to watch me perform magic tricks and that's what I do. There is some deceit, I admit, in *how* I perform my tricks."

"How's that?" asked Ben, slightly confused.

"Well, take the cloth, for example. I don't need the cloth to make the tree grow but without it, the 'trick' would cease to be just a 'trick,' and you would begin to believe I was actually doing real magic. Every one of my tricks has some element like this in it to allow the viewer to walk away impressed because they aren't sure how I crafted the illusion but still no closer than they were before to believing magic is real. Understand?"

Ben nodded slowly. He did understand but it was hard to wrap his mind around it nonetheless. His entire life he had believed only goblins possessed magical abilities. It was even a small source of pride, in a world dominated by humans, that his own kind, regardless of how estranged he was from them, could do something the humans couldn't.

"Are you alright?" asked Clara, putting a hand on his arm, making him startle a bit.

"Yes, sorry, I was just thinking," he said. "So, are you able to do magic, too?"

Clara grinned and raised an eyebrow. "Perhaps . . ." she said nonchalantly.

"She's . . . learning," interjected Plumstone before she could say more.

There was another brief silence and then the magician slapped his legs, marking the end of the conversation. "Now, I think we should get some sleep."

Sleep? Ben couldn't possibly imagine how

he could get any sleep now after all he had just learned. However, no sooner had he thought this than his eyes began to feel heavy.

It wasn't long until sleep did overcome him, and he woke several hours later around noon. Clara was reading a book quietly and Plumstone looked as though he were focusing very hard on a particular spot behind Ben's head.

Ben turned around and, seeing nothing, returned his gaze to the magician again. "Is something the matter?" he asked.

Plumstone's eyes flicked down to him and then back to the spot behind him.

Clara lowered her book and smiled. "He's trying not to be sick," she said. "He's not much for long carriage rides in the country."

"Oh, sorry," said Ben, quickly turning his attention to her, as though just looking at Plumstone would cause him to take ill.

"Why didn't we walk then?" he said in a

smaller voice.

"Too much to carry," said Clara, pointing a finger at the stacks of luggage behind them. "Besides, it would have taken ages."

"It's no matter," said Plumstone, not looking down at them. "We're nearly there, take a look."

Ben and Clara leaned out of their respective windows. On Ben's side, they passed a pond filled with more lily pads than he had ever seen in the whole of his life with brilliant white and yellow flowers that were in various stages of sprouting out of them. Up ahead was a hill, and through the trees, he could just make out a brick house. Within five minutes, they left the rough country road behind and had come upon a lovely brick street with large homes lining either side.

Ben and Clara took turns looking out their windows and then switching so that they could see as many of the beautiful homes as they could. Off to the north, Ben could see the spire of a white church.

"McKendree College," said Plumstone, who had calmed considerably since they had arrived in town and noticed Ben staring. "Oldest college in the region, I believe."

"Really?" asked Ben, curious.

"Oh yes," returned Plumstone. "It's a fascinating little town, Dickens, and I think you're really going to appreciate where we're staying."

The carriage rolled along down the streets, the horse's hooves clopping distinctively off of the bricks. They passed a police station and a library and then came to a stop.

The driver jumped down off of his seat and opened the door for them. He held out a hand to help Clara out and then moved to the back and began unloading their baggage.

When the dust settled, Plumstone pointed a little farther down the street to a charming building with red-painted siding.

"That's where we'll be staying. We should drop our luggage off and then we can explore the town a bit and get a bite to eat."

They all hefted their bags and began to walk. Now that the sound of horses' hooves clopping on brick had begun to fade into the distance, other sounds reached Ben's ears. Most notable of all was the birdsong. The town was ensconced in it. He looked to the trees and began to notice red cardinals, orange-breasted robins, yellow and gray chickadees, and blue jays flittering among them. A small hummingbird darted directly in front of them, its wings beating so fast that they were barely visible.

A group of children laughed and raced down the streets rolling makeshift hoops made from old bicycle rims. Women in large dresses and bonnets pushed prams up and down the sidewalks and shoppers bustled from store to store laden with sacks of goods.

"Do you know why this town is called Dickens, Ben?" asked Plumstone.

Ben shook his head.

"It's because a man by that name visited here once, oh, about sixty years ago. Stayed in the same inn that we are. He was a writer and he sort of took to the place. After he left, the town decided to rename itself. Used to be named after some country in the Near East, I believe."

Expecting him to continue, Ben waited for a moment. As he waited, though, the words began to sink in. A writer who shared the same name as the town from sixty years ago.

"You don't mean . . ."

Plumstone cracked a wide smile. "The one and the same!"

Ben was incredulous. "Charles Dickens, *the* Charles Dickens visited this little town? *And* he stayed in the same inn that I'm looking at right now?"

"He did indeed," said Plumstone. "I knew you'd like it."

They stopped in front of the red-sided inn and Ben read the sign hanging above the door.

10.
THE OLD SAILOR

"The Mermaid Inn," he read aloud. "That seems a bit of an odd name for an inn not on the coast."

"The proprietor was a sailor in a past life," explained Plumstone. "He claims to have spotted a mermaid during one of his sea voyages and named this inn after her."

"He saw a mermaid?" asked Ben, interested.

"Most likely a manatee," piped in Clara.

"Oh, I wouldn't be so sure," said Plumstone disapprovingly at the suggestion. "I know the sea does strange things to a man's mind, but I would hope he would have wits enough to tell the difference between a mermaid and a manatee."

The magician and his apprentice argued another minute or so about this while Ben studied the building, imagining the great writer standing in front of this very building, possibly on the very brick Ben was now standing on. It was a wondrous thought.

Their argument settled, at least for now, Plumstone strode forward and opened the door, motioning for Ben to enter. "After you."

Ben stepped through the door and into a foyer that contained an ornately carved staircase hugging the left wall. A small crystal chandelier, which was already lit even though it was hours till sunset, hung from the ceiling. The walls were covered in a blue and silver nautical themed wallpaper consisting of anchors, ship's wheels, and the namesake of the inn, mermaids. Straight ahead through double doors looked to be a kitchen and to the right was a large arched opening that led into a parlor.

It was a room much like those in Plumstone's house, comfortable wingback chairs, a sofa, bookshelves, and a fireplace at the heart of it all, which had a fire crackling merrily.

Lounging on the sofa was a man, who Ben assumed to be the proprietor. The man was striking and not just for his appearance, but for how that appearance was seemingly completely at odds with the otherwise pristine and well-kept inn in which he resided.

The first thing Ben noticed was the bright mustard yellow stocking cap that the man wore on his head. It was something that would have identified him from a mile away. The skin on his face was hard and wrinkled, tanned a permanent leathery reddish-brown from years at sea. He had a full, white beard and an unlit cigarette dangled from a corner of his mouth. He wore a white shirt that hung loosely on his scrawny body and a blue and white striped scarf wrapped around his neck.

He was staring straight at Ben as the small party entered, though it was not a look that made the goblin feel uncomfortable. It was simply a look of inquiry and curiosity — there was no disgust or fear there.

Plumstone stepped forward and boisterously greeted the man.

"Lyman, you old sea dog, it's good to see you!"

The old man looked up from Ben as though he had only just realized that the goblin had not been the only one to enter through his door.

"Percival?" he said in a voice that sounded much younger than his appearance would have indicated. "Do my old ears hear the voice of that charlatan street performer, Percival Plumstone?"

"Pish posh, you and I both know you're not as old as you seem," said Plumstone with a wink. He closed the distance and clasped hands with the old sailor.

Lyman stood and diverted his gaze to Clara, his smile widening.

"Miss Clara, you're still stuck with this odd fellow?"

"I'm afraid so," she said, matching his grin. She then turned to Ben and pulled him forward.

"This is our friend Ben. We're taking him to . . . well, you know where, tonight."

Lyman's eyes widened. "Are you now? It's a strange sight to find a goblin traveling with a pair of folks such as yourselves. Strange sight indeed." He pulled at his beard as though considering this thought for a moment before pressing on. Then he stepped forward and offered a hand. "Lyman Gore, pleased to meet you, mate."

Ben warily reached up and took his hand. "Ben Tamm."

The sailor nodded and began pulling at his beard again. "Tamm, eh? Hmm, can't say as I know any goblins called Tamm. I suppose you're not from around here?"

"No, sir. I was born in Jotunfell."

"Indeed." He grunted and then slapped his legs. "Well now, if you're to be going down to the, uh, well you know where, we'd best get you some rooms and a meal before heading out."

He turned and strode over to a desk in the foyer. He scratched a couple marks in a ledger and then reached into a drawer, producing several keys.

"Your usual rooms," he said, handing keys to Plumstone and Clara. "And for you, young master goblin."

He held out the last key to Ben.

"Right!" said Plumstone. "Let's take some time to get freshened up. We'll meet back down here in a half hour, have a bite to eat, and see some of the town before heading out."

Ben hefted his bag and followed Plumstone up the stairs. Lyman disappeared into another room that Ben guessed to be the kitchen.

At the top of the stairs, Plumstone pointed out Ben's room to him before entering his own. Ben inserted the key into the lock and opened the door.

The room was only slighter larger than his own quarters in the lighthouse but much more nicely furnished. It had a bed large enough for two, a night table, dresser, and a plush armchair sitting in front of one of the two windows.

Ben set down his satchel, pulled out some fresh clothes, and changed into them. Then he collapsed in the armchair and took in the view of the street below while quietly reflecting on his day.

A half of an hour later, he and Plumstone

returned downstairs and found Clara sitting in the parlor. She was reading a book — *The Old Curiosity Shop* by Charles Dickens — when they arrived.

"They have his full catalog of works here," she said, holding up the book.

"I would expect nothing less in this town," said Plumstone, taking a seat beside her.

A short while later, Lyman returned and beckoned them all to lunch. He served fried fish, boiled potatoes, green beans, and slightly stale bread. To a hungry goblin, it was a feast fit for kings. After they were sufficiently fed, they bid the innkeeper goodbye and set about touring the town.

11.
THE UNSEEN MARKET

For the next few hours, they made their way up and down the main street of Dickens, stopping into nearly every shop they passed. Ben got his first ice cream soda in the corner pharmacy. Plumstone picked up a few books at the bookshop and even bought Ben his own copy of *The Old Curiosity Shop* to commemorate his first trip to the town. Clara bought nothing but seemed to enjoy herself just the same.

When they had gone the length of the street on one side and then come back up the other, they found themselves back at the Mermaid Inn. Plumstone carried all of their purchases inside and dropped them off in their rooms before they set off for the market.

They were going to make the trip on foot as the magician had had enough carriage riding for one day. The prairie where the Unseen Market was held was only a couple miles away, and that coupled with pleasant, warm weather, promised to make for a nice walk.

The warm afternoon, however, as it is wont to do in early spring, soon turned into a cool evening. By the time they arrived at nearly half past nine o'clock, Ben wished that he had packed his cloak and scarf.

They came upon the precipice of a hill and Plumstone put out their lantern. All around them was silence. As it was the night of a new moon, the sky and the land below were completely cloaked in darkness. Ben's goblin eyes adjusted to the dark quicker than humans but even he was practically blind.

Then up ahead, the sound of a stick snapping in half could be heard. It was followed by footsteps crunching the earth and it seemed to be growing nearer.

Ben could barely make out the outlines of his companions, but he could tell that they weren't moving and didn't appear to be concerned by this approaching sound.

"Beautiful moon," said Plumstone.

"Everyone is a moon . . ." replied the stranger in a hoarse whisper.

". . . and has a dark side which he never shows to anybody," finished Plumstone.

A light suddenly lit up the area and Ben could see the stranger holding a now-lit lantern. The light that shone from it emitted an eerie purple glow. The stranger's face was hidden in the shadow of a hooded cloak, which he wrapped around himself tightly, save for the hand holding the lantern.

"Good evening, Simon," said Plumstone.

"Evening, Master Plumstone, good to see you again. I see you've brought your young apprentice," said Simon, his eyes and his lantern roving over the small group. Then they both stopped on Ben. "Who's the goblin?"

"A friend," said Plumstone, putting his hand on Ben's shoulder, as though this act of familiarity proved his statement.

Simon pulled back his hood a little and leaned down closer. His face was still mostly masked, but Ben could make out smooth, pale skin, thick bifocals, and what looked like a mostly hairless head. Simon raised an eyebrow. "Is that so? This his first market?"

"It is," said Ben, wanting to speak for himself.

Simon paused a little and looked him over some more. "Well, you'll need to listen to the rules before I can let you proceed."

Ben nodded his agreement and Simon

cleared his throat.

"Right then. The rules are these . . . be civil and don't steal."

Ben waited for more but after several moments of silence, he realized there was no more. "That seems simple enough," he said.

Simon scoffed. "Seems so, doesn't it? You'd be surprised how hard it can be for some folks. Well then, you've been warned, so, off with you now."

Simon pulled his hood forward again and nodded. He held out the purple-lighted lantern, which the magician took before descending the hill with Ben and Clara in tow.

They were halfway down the hill and below was a large, flat prairie that appeared to be completely abandoned. However, as they drew nearer, a feint glow began to emanate from a spot nearly one hundred yards or so away. As they walked closer to the glow, it widened and spread and soon that single light had become several lights. When they had halved the distance, the glow revealed itself to be a collection of hundreds of lanterns spread around dozens of tents and wagons, each of them sending out the same purple light.

"Welcome to the Unseen Market," said Plumstone, and Ben realized it was the first time he had heard the magician utter those words in a normal tone rather than a whisper.

It was the most marvelous sight that Ben had ever seen. Now that he was closer, he could see that each and every tent had its own style and personality. Some were tall and peaked, some were short and long, some were blue with silver stars, and one even seemed to be made entirely of lantern light.

There were many wagons as well, mostly covered, some with cloth like the old settlers would have used, though most were covered with wooden planks and had doors and windows, like little houses on wheels.

Hundreds of people moved and crowded down the cramped aisles, and through the din of their voices could be heard music from every direction. Violins, lutes, pipes, flutes, and many more Ben couldn't identify rang out their songs. Occasionally, fireworks would burst from the ground and explode in a burst of color and sound above their heads, drawing oohs and aahs from the onlookers.

"How . . . ?"

"Let's just say that goblins aren't the only ones capable of creating illusions. Though I should say that your kind does it purely with the power of the mind, whereas humans require certain spells and enchantments."

He held up the lantern.

"This lantern," he said, indicating it, "shines an anti-illusory light that reveals things which are normally hidden."

"Amazing," said Ben in a barely audible whisper.

"Come," said Plumstone, putting an arm around Ben's shoulder. "I always feel the best way to learn about something is to dive right in; explore from the inside!"

As they drew nearer, Ben was fascinated with all of the different wares on display. Some, like the specialty plants and minerals used in alchemy, the enchanted weapons, and the books of spells, he recognized from the market in Jotunfell.

Most of the items, though, were entirely new. There were pendants and amulets that emitted an eerie luminescence, cauldrons of every shape, size, and material, potions that glowed every color of the rainbow, and exotic animals that were merely the stuff of legends to the vast majority of the world's inhabitants. And, of course, as with any mass gathering of humans, there was food: cakes and pies, sugared pecans, kettle corn, drinking chocolates, hot and cold teas, and a strange, steaming blue drink that smelled very similar to coffee mixed with cooked blueberries.

"Now, let's see," Plumstone was saying to Clara, "where was that book peddler that we ran into last time?"

"The one who sold you the fake Shakespeare folio?" she asked.

Plumstone's face grew slightly red, and he frowned. "No, definitely not him. If my entreaties were properly respected, he won't be showing his face at any market in middle America for quite some time."

"There are other markets?" asked Ben.

"Well, of course!" said Clara. "You didn't think we were so special to have the only one in the world, did you?"

Ben flushed and shrugged. "I suppose I hadn't really thought about it."

He diverted his eyes and suddenly his face grew deathly pale.

Both Plumstone and Clara noticed and

looked in the direction he was.

"What's wrong?" asked Clara, concern all over her face.

"Goblins," said Ben.

Sure enough, a trio of green hill goblins could be seen a few rows of tents away. They looked angered at being in such close proximity to humans.

"I recognize them," said Ben, his anxiety rising, "Let's just say it wouldn't be good if they noticed me."

"Right," said Plumstone without inquiring further, which Ben was happy for. He looked around and then said, "Aha! Wait here."

He strode away to a nearby stall and returned less than a minute later with a crimson piece of fabric draped over one arm.

"Here," he said. "Try this on."

He took the fabric in both hands and put it around the goblin's shoulders. Ben reached up and fastened the cloak's clasp and pulled the hood over his head. It was a deep hood like the one Simon had worn, and Ben's face practically disappeared into its depths.

"Perfect!" said Clara. "*I* barely even recognize you!"

"Thank you," said Ben to Plumstone. "How much do I owe you?"

"Consider it a gift," said the magician, smiling, "to remember your first market!"

"Thank you," repeated Ben, and he truly meant it. He hadn't worn any article of clothing this fine since he had left Jotunfell and even then, his clothes had been of a much lesser quality than his brothers'.

"Well, that's settled!" said Plumstone. "Now, I think we should split up and cover more ground. You two look for any book peddlers you can find and see about that book. I'll go meet with a few acquaintances of mine who may know something about the, um, well, something about the item that I'm looking for."

Ben wanted to ask what exactly the item was, but Clara spoke first.

"Meet back here in an hour?"

"Better make it two," said Plumstone. "I don't expect my conversations to be brief."

They agreed and went their separate ways. Before they went too far, though, Clara insisted they stop and get a little nourishment. Ten minutes later, they emerged with pieces of pie in one hand — cherry for Ben, peach for Clara — and large mugs of the hot blue drink in the other.

"It tastes like coffee, too," said Ben, taking slow sips, "but better!"

Clara laughed. "That's why we call it blue coffee! It has a real name, but no one uses it."

The first two book peddlers they came across only dealt in magical tomes, and each seemed offended when they asked about *Gobelin Sagas*, a common storybook. The third had never heard of the book, and the fourth and fifth said they had heard of it but hadn't seen a copy on the market in years.

When they arrived at the tent of the sixth book peddler, Ben had to look twice. Sure enough, it was the very same peddler who had sold Ben books for years back in Jotunfell and had assisted in Ben's liberation nearly a year and a half earlier.

Ben approached him cautiously and after glancing around, drew back his hood slightly. The peddler's face lit up upon seeing him. However, up close, that face wasn't exactly as Ben had remembered it. It was now missing an eye and a large scar split the otherwise smooth blueish skin above and beneath it.

"How did you . . ." began Ben, but the peddler held up a hand.

"Don't you worry about it," he said. "I'm a traveling merchant and with that occupation comes the risk of danger."

"But, it wasn't because of . . . me, was it?"

The peddler sighed but said nothing, which to Ben was as good as an affirmation.

Ben began to speak but the peddler held up a hand again.

"I would do everything the same if I had it to do over again," he said. "Seeing you here, in the close company of that human girl, only affirms that."

Ben was silent for a moment as he wrestled with the guilt that he still felt, despite the reassurances. "Which one of them was it?" he asked.

"Does it matter?" asked the peddler.

Ben wanted to shout out that yes, it did matter, and he even thought about writing to his father and demanding punishment be dealt to the one who did this . . . but ultimately, he knew it was all futile.

"No, I suppose not," he said.

The peddler smiled. "I'm alright, truly. It makes me look a little tougher, don't you think?

I've certainly had less problems with highwaymen since I lost the eye."

He chuckled, and Ben forced a weak smile.

"So, how can I help you tonight? Are you searching for anything specific or just browsing like the old days?"

Clara stepped up beside Ben and her presence helped clear his mind.

"We're looking for a book called *Gobelin Sags*," she said. "We haven't had much luck so far, and it doesn't look like there are too many other chances to find it."

The peddler shook his head. "Of all the books you could have asked me for, it had to be that one," he said. "I'm sorry, young lady, but I know for a fact that you won't find that book among my wares or anyone else's here."

"Really?" asked Clara, a frown creasing her forehead. "Why's that?"

"Because it no longer exists, at least, not to my knowledge," he said and then he turned to

Ben. "Years ago, your great-grandfather sent out several parties of goblins in search of that very book. Anywhere they found a copy, it was seized and burned on the spot. My father, whose trade I have inherited, personally had at least ten copies seized from his wagon."

"Why would they do that?" asked Ben and Clara, nearly at the same time.

The peddler shrugged. "No one knows the exact reason, but most speculated that there was some piece of information hidden among the stories in that book that your great-grandfather didn't want anyone to see, whether it be humans or goblins alike."

Ben's eyes grew wide as a scene from his childhood suddenly played itself across his mind's eye. He was eight or nine, and it was late at night. He had snuck into the library after hours and entered the restricted section, which was closed off to everyone except for the librarian himself and the Hob. The reason why it was restricted was why Ben loved it so much. It was chock-full of books written by human authors. When Ben had asked the librarian why they were even there, the librarian had muttered something about knowing your enemy and refused to say any more.

After that, Ben had made that section of the library a frequent after-hours haunt. The night before, he had been reading *Robinson Crusoe* and he couldn't wait to pick back up on the marooned man's adventures.

Earlier in the day, he had unlocked one of the upper-story windows and once the sky grew dark, he climbed the stone wall to the window and crept inside. The restricted section was locked but Ben had long ago made a copy of the key. He stopped and listened for the librarian, which was mostly just a precaution, as he knew that once the library was closed for the night, the librarian rarely left his chambers in the backroom of the building.

Robinson Crusoe had just begun to carve out his canoe when Ben heard four sounds that drew his attention. The first was a knock on the front door. The second was the shuffling of the librarian's feet. The third was the front door opening, and the fourth was his father's voice.

This last sound made Ben grow cold all over, and he suddenly wished that he had just gone to bed as he should have. Was his father here for him? Did he know that Ben wasn't at home? He had never visited his rooms before or even shown any inclination to speak to his son more than the occasional stiff "hello." Why start now of all nights?

Ben's fear was momentarily quelled when he heard the words that his father and the librarian were speaking.

"I am in need of a book," came the voice of the Hob, flat with no emotion attached to it.

"Of course, of course," replied the librarian. "Does your lordship have any particular book in mind?"

"I highly doubt that I would venture out in the middle of the night if I did not have a particular book in mind," said the Hob.

"Of course, you wouldn't, my lord, forgive me for asking."

There was a brief silence and then his father's voice again. "Might I actually enter, or do you mean to keep me on your doorstep to catch a chill?"

More feet shuffling.

"Forgive me again, my lord. How foolish of me. Please, come in."

The sound of the door closing and the bolts being drawn.

"Now, which book may I have the pleasure of fetching for you, my lord?"

"It is an old book of which I have recently learned of in my father's journals. It is called *Gobelin Sagas*."

Another silence.

"I . . . I'm sorry, my lord, but I know for a fact that I have no book of that name here."

"You don't wish to check first before making such a claim?" asked the Hob.

The librarian began to whisper, and Ben listened closer, holding his breath in an attempt to hear. All he heard, though, was his father's angered shouts and the door being thrown open again, with the librarian groveling in his wake.

As Ben emerged from his reverie, he realized that the peddler was eyeing him warily and he wondered how long he had been silently lost in his memories.

"Though it's none of my business, I do find myself wondering . . . how exactly did you even hear of this book? It's been erased from history for decades."

Ben hesitated, not sure if it was smart to reveal the location of perhaps the only remaining copy of the book, but just looking at the peddler's scarred face reminded Ben that he could probably be trusted.

"The library in Saint Louis. I found a copy there with . . . help from a friend."

The peddler's eyes widened. "Did you now? That's most interesting. Might I ask, why not just read that copy?"

Ben sighed. "If only I could, but I'm not allowed in the library . . ."

". . . because you're a goblin," finished the peddler. "I see. Well, my friend, I wish I could assist you in finding it but . . ." his words trailed off, the end of the sentence being unnecessary. "Is there anything else I can help you with?" the peddler asked after a brief pause.

"Do you have the time?" asked Clara.

The peddler reached into his pocket and pulled out his fob watch. "Nearly a quarter past midnight," he said.

Clara grabbed Ben's arm. "We're late!" she said.

Ben and Clara bid the peddler thanks and

farewell, and they hurried off to meet Plumstone.

The peddler watched them go with a proud smile.

"Until next we meet, my friend."

12.
EMPTY HANDED

Plumstone was waiting for them when they arrived ten minutes later, but he wasn't alone. A tall man was speaking with him. His back was facing Ben and Clara, but the goblin immediately recognized the bright yellow stocking cap.

"Is that Mr. Gore?" he asked.

Clara smiled coyly but said nothing.

As they approached, the man in the yellow cap turned around and Ben was taken aback. The man certainly looked like the innkeeper.

He even wore the same clothes and hat as the innkeeper. However, this man was at least fifty years younger, his skin was smooth and pale, his beard was a fiery orange, and he stood perfectly erect, making him at least a foot taller than the man Ben had met earlier that afternoon.

"Ah, you're back," said Plumstone as they approached. "Look who I ran into."

"Lyman, why didn't you tell us you were coming tonight?" asked Clara. "We could have traveled together."

"And a fine thing it would have been, too, my lady," said Lyman jovially. "Though to tell you the truth, I hadn't really made up my mind to come until a minute before I came."

"Did you have any success finding the book?" asked Plumstone.

Clara shook her head and sighed. "No, and I don't think we will either."

"Why's that?"

"Ben, do you want to tell him?" she asked.

They waited, but Ben didn't reply. He couldn't take his eyes off of Lyman and was still standing with a look of utter disbelief on his face.

"Ben?" Clara prodded, elbowing him gently in the ribs.

Ben jumped and turned to her abruptly. "What's that? Did you say something?"

"Is everything alright, little mate? I hardly recognized you underneath that cloak." Lyman's voice caused Ben to jump and he cautiously turned back to the sailor.

"You . . . you're . . ."

Lyman stared at Ben for a moment and then burst into uproarious laughter.

"You look as though you've seen a ghost! Easy now, boy. Look around you and think about where we are."

Ben slowly turned his head from side to side and took in the surroundings.

"Why, I'd reckon there's not a soul here what come with his normal looks intact," he said. "Present company excluded, of course."

"You mean, it's magic?" asked Ben cautiously.

"Of course! I change my appearance more than a baby changes his bedclothes!"

Ben still looked skeptical and Lyman fell into further fits of laughter.

Clara linked her arm into Ben's.

"It's alright," she said. "He's telling the truth. We probably should have warned you, but we've known him for a long time and it's just commonplace now."

Ben nodded. Her touch seemed to break his stupor a little and he forced himself to relax.

"So, now back to business," she said, returning her attention to Plumstone. "What about you, did you find what you were looking for?"

Now it was the magician's turn to shake his

head and sigh.

"No. I had a few potential leads but none of them panned out. There's rumors of one being spotted out west and I have someone checking on it," he said, "but we won't find anything out most likely until the next market at the earliest."

"What was it that you were looking for?" asked Ben, realizing that Plumstone had never actually shared what the object of his search had been.

Plumstone looked around and then leaned in conspiratorially, motioning the others to do the same.

When they were all standing huddled together, Plumstone said in a hushed voice, "A mirage mask."

Clara exchanged a quick glance with him as he said it, though the others didn't notice.

Lyman let out a slow whistle. "That's not exactly a common item, even around here."

"Have you seen or heard of any lately?"

asked Plumstone to the sailor.

Lyman shook his head and twirled the cigarette with his tongue. "Nah, not for some time. Long before I met you, I can tell you that."

Ben cleared his throat and the other three turned to him. "Sorry to interrupt, but what exactly is a mirage mask?"

"An old goblin trick," said Lyman. "Sneaky little buggers – no offense to you, of course – used 'em a lot a while back. Not so common now, I think they realized humans were catching on."

"Yes, but what do they do?" asked Ben, trying not to sound as impatient as he felt.

"In the simplest terms, they turn a goblin into a human, or rather make them appear to be human," explained Plumstone. "They truly are a master work, being able to place an illusion into a physical object."

Ben shook his head. "Why would they want to appear to be human? They hate humans."

"For mischief, of course," said Lyman. "Think of all the trouble they could cause if they could blend in easily without the strain of maintaining an illusion."

"Wow, that *would* have been something, wouldn't it?" remarked Ben wistfully.

Plumstone looked crestfallen. "I'm sorry, Ben, it's the only thing I could think of that would get you into that library as soon as possible."

Ben tried to smile but felt it falter before it had even had a chance to start. Plumstone quickly tried to change the subject.

"What about that book again?" he asked.

Ben paused and then repeated what the book peddler had told them about his great-grandfather's purge.

"That's some irony for you!" said Lyman with another long whistle.

"So, it was all for nothing," said Clara. "I'm so sorry to get your hopes up, Ben."

"It's not your fault," he said. "You did more than most anyone else I've ever known would have done to help me."

Plumstone was still silent, but he wore a look of determination.

13.
GHOST STORY

They refilled their drinks, grabbed some food for the road, and set off on the long walk back to Dickens. They were joined this time by Lyman Gore, who proved to be a boisterous companion. Even though Ben was used to staying awake all night long, it was usually after at least half of a day sleeping. Even with the several cups of blue coffee and a full stomach, the couple hours he had managed to sleep in the carriage weren't enough to keep his eyes and limbs from feeling heavy.

Lyman and Clara led the pack and Plumstone dropped back to walk beside Ben, who had begun to lag behind.

"You alright?"

Ben rubbed his eyes and yawned loudly. "I'll be fine."

Plumstone looked at him skeptically. "I'm really sorry this didn't work out for you."

"It's alright," said Ben. "Traveling here, seeing the market, meeting an old friend . . . it was worth the coming."

"Still, doesn't get you any closer to that book."

"That's true." Ben sighed. "Maybe it's just not meant to be."

Plumstone arched an eyebrow. "You don't really believe that, do you?"

Ben shrugged and then shook his head. "No, but that's what people say when things don't work out the way they wanted."

"So, tell me again, why does this book mean so much to you?"

Ben looked up at the dark circle where the moon was currently hidden by the earth's shadow. He took a breath and made a decision.

"My name isn't Ben Tamm ... it's Ben Tamorensson. My father ... is the Hob of Jotunfell."

Plumstone stopped dead in his tracks. Ben stopped walking as well and turned back to him. "I take it you've heard of my father."

The magician nodded. Ben waited for more, but when no response came, he continued.

"My entire life I thought that I was the only goblin like me, just a mistake, born wrong somehow. Three months ago, not long after you and I met for the first time, my brother came for me and brought me to my father. I was prepared for the worst but not at all prepared for what ended up happening.

"As it happens, my father, whom I grew up

fearing and whom all of goblinkind admire and respect, is just like me."

Plumstone's brow began to crease, and he shook his head. "No, that can't be right," he said. "I've met him, and he was worse than the others."

"You've met him?"

Plumstone didn't respond.

"Well, regardless, it's just as I said. He's been hiding it his entire life."

"How is that possible? Wouldn't his *kenna* give him away?"

Ben stopped and stared at his companion.

"How do you know what *kenna* is? I thought only goblins knew that."

Plumstone hesitated and then said, "Well, I don't know all the intricacies of it but during my travels, I've heard it mentioned. Isn't it something like the ability to read minds?"

Ben wasn't sure about this answer, but it was late and his mind was groggy, so he let it go and pushed on.

"Not exactly, it's more like reading or sensing emotions. My grandfather taught him an old method to mask his *kenna* and he's kept it up for over fifty years."

"Unbelievable, I can only imagine the mental strength that would require," said Plumstone, obviously both stunned and impressed by this revelation.

"So, that's why I need to read that book. There's something in there that my grandfather didn't want the world to know about. I could feel it the moment I laid eyes on it. My father even wanted it, maybe for this very reason. He told me that someone can't be an anomaly if another exists in his image. There's a reason why we are the way we are. Who knows, maybe there's more of us out there somewhere?"

"Unbelievable," Plumstone repeated.

They fell silent then and, for the rest of the

journey, contented themselves to listen to the old sailor tell stories about life at sea. When they arrived back at the Mermaid Inn, they all promptly fell into bed and slept long, dreamless sleeps. It was near to noon by the time Ben finally awoke, feeling sore and weary but refreshed.

Plumstone and Clara were waiting downstairs in the dining room, where a cup of regular coffee and breakfast had been laid out for him.

"Good morning!" said Clara. "Sleep well?"

"Quite well, thank you, and you?"

Clara nodded enthusiastically. "Oh yes, I always sleep well here."

"Are you ready to leave after breakfast?" asked Plumstone.

"Yes, I think so," he said, remembering that Maribel was due to come back to the lighthouse that night.

Ben ate his breakfast while Plumstone

loaded up the carriage. When Ben was finished, he ran back to their room and fetched his satchel. He bid Lyman goodbye, and Plumstone secured his bag.

"Ben, would you mind doing me a quick favor?" asked Plumstone, tightening the rope.

"Of course."

The magician dug into his pockets and produced a few coins, which he handed to Ben.

"Run down to the pharmacy and pick me up today's paper, will you?"

Ben nodded and took the coins. He left the inn and raced down the street to the pharmacy he remembered walking past the day before. He walked in cautiously, prepared for the ensuing panic that usually followed unsuspecting humans when a goblin entered their midst, but to his surprise, no one seemed to pay him much mind.

He walked over to the stack of newspapers, grabbed the top one, and took it to the clerk.

"Just the paper, then? Can I tempt you with an ice cream or soda water?" asked the clerk. He was a large man with a bald head, mustache, and a friendly smile.

"Just the paper is all," said Ben, dropping the coins onto the counter.

"Very well." The clerk picked up the coins and began pressing buttons on his register. "Been in town long?"

"Just since yesterday. My friends and I stayed overnight at the Mermaid Inn."

"Uh huh, well that makes sense. Old Alfred treat you well?"

Ben frowned. "Alfred? No, I'm sorry, the man there is called Lyman . . . Lyman Gore."

It was as if all of the air had been sucked out the room at once and everyone fell silent.

Ben looked around to see every eye in the room staring at him. "What did I say?"

The clerk was frowning heavily at him but then began to chuckle.

"You're pulling my leg boy. Having a laugh my expense, are you?"

"I don't think so."

"Now listen, I've lived in this town my entire life," explained the clerk. "Lived here back before it was even called Dickens. Hell, I remember the festival we had to celebrate. This town loves a good festival."

"I'm sure it does," said Ben lamely.

"I know every man, woman, and child here. So, I think I know that the owner of the Mermaid Inn is a fellow by the name of Alfred Gore."

Ben was very confused at this point. Humans sure had a way of talking around a topic. "Maybe he just goes by Lyman?"

The clerk was shaking his head. "Lyman was his granddaddy, the original owner of the inn. He died about, oh, some fifty or so years back. Long before my time."

Ben felt an icy chill sweep up his back. His

brain had gone numb and at that moment, he just wanted to get out of there, away from the staring eyes and the cashier's words that seemed to linger on the air.

He took a couple steps back, slowly at first, and then he turned and fled from the store.

"Hey! You forgot your paper," the clerk called, but his words only hit the closing door as the goblin disappeared down the street.

❊ ❊ ❊

Ben climbed into the carriage and sat back hurriedly into his seat. He barely noticed the cold sweat that had broken out on his brow and was trickling down his face as he wrapped his arms around himself and stared blankly out the window.

Plumstone and Clara looked at each other and then back to their goblin friend. His emerald skin had turned the pale color of moss.

"Ben," said Clara slowly, reaching out a hand. When it briefly touched the skin on Ben's arm, he jumped and looked at them with wide eyes.

"Is everything alright?" asked Plumstone, knowing full well that it wasn't. No one behaved as Ben was if everything was alright.

Ben seemed to be having trouble focusing, but he was aware that his friends looked concerned. His mouth had gone dry, and try as he might, he was having trouble prying it open so that words could escape.

He swallowed hard and licked his lips enough to get out two words.

"Lyman . . . dead."

Once again, the magician and his apprentice exchanged glances, this time no longer questioning but knowing . . . knowing, and not completely sure what or how to say what needed to be said.

At last, Plumstone scooted across his seat so that he was facing Ben directly. He leaned forward and looked into Ben's eyes until he was satisfied that the goblin was listening.

"You're right. Lyman is dead. And that man in there is Lyman."

These words were not meant to calm or to comfort, but the first step in acceptance of a hard truth is taking away any room for your ever-wandering mind to create any extra, possibly more disturbing scenarios based around said truth.

"He died fifty-five years ago," Plumstone continued. "As you know, he was . . . is, a magician and a greater one by far than I am or probably will ever be. During his years of endless study in his craft, he discovered a secret — a secret about the very essence of life as we know it. He found that we — humans, goblins, and every other living creature that lives and breathes — are made up of two parts."

Plumstone held up two fingers. He pointed to his index finger. "The first is the body, our physical presence, and the body is connected intricately to the earth we live on."

He pointed to his other finger. "The second is the spirit, our emotional presence, the essence of life itself. Without a spirit, the body is just a lifeless piece of meat with no purpose or reason.

"The secret that he discovered was that when the body dies, the spirit ascends to another plane of existence and leaves our world behind. However, with the help of very advanced magic, he found a way to tie the spirit to the earth even after the body dies, thereby allowing the spirit to live on indefinitely."

Plumstone stopped and waited.

The fog that had clouded Ben's mind, though, had begun to dissipate ever since the magician had looked at him so directly, almost as though he had used magic on him to help calm his nerves and clear his head.

Ben heard every word and was now processing those words. If you or I had been in his position and heard those exact words, we probably would not have been able to make sense of them, at least not in a way that would allow our minds to believe them, to take them as a factual truth. And believe me, there is a difference between factual and non-factual truths, for a truth alone is just something our minds allow us to believe, regardless of how factual they really are.

So, it was a lucky thing then that Ben was, in fact, a goblin. A goblin who had grown up in a city that not only believed in the existence of magic but practiced it every day. A goblin who had witnessed the magic of illusion on more occasions than he could count. And so, it didn't take long before he allowed himself to believe Plumstone's words.

"So, if a spirit is separate from a body," Ben began slowly, "and a body is the physical presence, then why can I see him?"

Plumstone grinned. "As I said, he's a greater

magician than I. It took him several years, as he tells it, to create a corporeal manifestation of himself, but eventually he did it. That's how he changed his appearance from a crooked old man to the tall strapping sailor you saw last night."

Ben didn't understand it, but he also knew that he didn't need to completely understand it to believe it.

"And so, he's been posing as his relations ever since, which is why the townsfolk think his name is Alfred?"

"Precisely," said Plumstone. "He changes his name every thirty years or so, along with his appearance."

"Why didn't you tell me before?"

"Because we were afraid you would react, well, like this," said Clara with a nervous chuckle.

Ben forced a crooked smile and wiped his brow.

"Alright, enough ghost stories," said Plumstone, tapping the ceiling of the carriage. "Let's be off. We have a long ride ahead and I have much to think about on the way."

The driver whipped the reigns and the carriage slowly pulled into motion. Ben looked out the window at the Mermaid Inn, envisioning Lyman Gore sitting on the sofa, pretending to be alive and fooling the whole town at the same time. If only they knew that their innkeeper was truly a ghost.

14.
The Goblin's Secret

Their carriage rolled back across the Eads Bridge into Saint Louis in the mid-afternoon. The sun was high in the sky but was interrupted by frequent gray clouds that promised a rain-soaked evening to come. Instead of stopping at the riverfront to let Ben off, the carriage continued west toward Lafayette Park.

During the ride, Plumstone had not said a word, instead staring pensively out of the side window, still as a statue. He didn't look as affected by the rocking motion of the carriage as he had on the trip to Dickens the day before.

They came to a stop directly in front of the magician's front door. The driver opened the door for them before untying their luggage. Ten minutes later, they were alone again in the large house, the clopping of the carriage horses' hooves echoing off into the distance.

Plumstone closed the door and locked it before motioning Ben and Clara to follow him. He led them upstairs, down a hallway, and up more stairs to the tower library, where he once again closed the door behind them and locked it with a large brass key, which he quickly replaced in his pocket.

"Please, sit," he said to Ben, indicating one of the plush chairs that had been piled with books.

Clara helped Ben clear it off and then she began to sit in the chair next to him, but Plumstone held out a hand.

"If you wouldn't mind, could you please

come stand by me?"

Clara looked at him with a curious eye but shrugged her shoulders and strode over to stand at the magician's side.

"What's this about?" asked Ben, who was beginning to get worried.

Plumstone seemed to be considering his words carefully and was in no hurry to begin speaking but finally, he took a deep breath and plunged onward.

"Ben, we, Clara and I, haven't been entirely honest with you."

Clara immediately turned and gaped at him. She apparently knew exactly what he was about already.

"Are you ghosts, too?" asked Ben with a nervous chuckle, hoping silently that he was wrong. He wasn't sure how many more ghosts he could handle in one day.

Plumstone shook his head and wiped his brow.

"No, no," he said, his voice quavering. "But, like Master Gore, we also aren't exactly what we seem."

Ben didn't realize he was doing it, but his body had grown tense and rigid, bracing itself for whatever Plumstone would say next.

"When you first told me your problem of needing to be able to freely walk amongst humans without the constant prejudices that followed you relentlessly around everywhere you went, I knew what the answer was. As you are not magically-inclined like the majority of your species, there really is only one answer."

Clara's eyes had increasingly grown wider with each word that the magician spoke. It was clear that she couldn't believe that he was actually uttering them aloud.

"The mirage mask," he continued. "I hoped to find one at the market, but I was already quite certain that I wouldn't find one there. They are, as I said, very rare. I was additionally hopeful that you would be able to find your book and we could leave it all at that. Even after we both found failure in our searches, I was still unsure of how to proceed. However, what you told me about your father has swayed my mind."

At this, he turned to Clara. "I know we made a pact long ago to never tell anyone regardless of the circumstances, but this is a situation that even I could never have fathomed, and I think we must make an exception. However, I will only do so if you agree."

Clara stared at him, though it was obvious that she wasn't really looking at him. Finally, she nodded and sighed. "Well, I suppose it's easier than my next suggestion of copying the whole book for him by hand," she said with a small grin. "So, I agree."

Plumstone smiled and wrapped his arms around her in an embrace, and Ben realized it was the first time he had ever seen them show any sort of emotion for each other.

The magician turned back to Ben and Clara faced him as well. The two held hands tightly and their free hands went to their faces. It's hard to describe exactly what happened next and even Ben, who was sitting not five feet away from them, would have been able to tell it in much detail, but one second a human man and a human girl stood before him and the next second, they had changed completely, and two entirely different figures had replaced them.

They were now closer in height to each other; the color of their skin had changed from the pale pallor of a white peach to something closer to a blueberry; and their ears . . .

"Y . . . you're goblins."

Plumstone, who, despite his changed skin color, still looked very much like himself, or at least the himself that Ben had known, slowly nodded.

"It's true, and we're frost goblins actually.

Well, at least partially."

"Partially?"

"Our father was a frost goblin and our mother was a human," said Clara, whose dark black hair was now streaked with violet.

"Our father?" At this point, Ben didn't feel he was capable of too many words at once and there were too many questions to ask.

Clara walked over and sat beside him. "He's my brother," she said. "When we first started using the masks, we still posed as siblings but after living among humans for a short while, we found it more profitable and believable to be magician and apprentice instead."

Ben closed his eyes and buried his head in his hands. "I don't understand, this is a lot to take in."

"I realize that," said Plumstone, approaching and kneeling beside his chair. "I considered waiting to tell you, but I began to feel as though the longer you knew us as humans, the more deceived you would feel when we finally told you the truth.

"Our story is long but not over-complicated, and I will tell you more in time. For now, the important parts are that we were both born, as my sister said, to a goblin father and a human mother. Frost goblins, as you know, are less hostile toward humans and our mother was a unique spirit, capable of warming even the iciest of hearts. So, it was no great surprise that my father fell for her. When they both died, we were left alone, not welcome among either humans or goblins because both species saw us as unnatural half-breeds."

"Our father was a great magician," continued Clara, "and he had been searching for the mirage masks ever since Percy was born. He and mother didn't mind being outcasts because they had each other, but he knew that we wouldn't be so eager to spend the rest of our lives in seclusion."

"He found one before he died," said Plumstone, holding his mask out to Ben, who took it hesitantly. It didn't look like anything special, just an ordinary wooden mask with two circular holes for eyes and another circle on the forehead with a runic symbol carved into it.

"We found the other together," said Clara, holding up her own.

Ben turned the mask over in his hands, taking in every detail. It wasn't until the light streaming in from the window caught it at the right angle that he noticed a soft reflective purple glow that shimmered wherever the light touched it.

"The color of magic," said Plumstone, reading Ben's thoughts. "It's why I chose my surname when we decided to become human."

"How many are there?" asked Ben.

Plumstone tilted his head and ran a hand over the mask. "No one really knows. As I said before, they're a master work of illusion, so I wouldn't imagine there would be too many. It took the better part of my father's life to find the one, and the better part of my life to find the other, so who knows how long it could be before we find a third," he said. "However, I laid the groundwork for finding another at the market last night. The right people know I'm looking."

Ben nodded and handed the mask back to the magician, but instead of taking it back, he pushed it back toward Ben.

"In the meantime, we'll share."

15.
BEN THE HUMAN

On the walk back to the lighthouse, Ben passed the library. It was early evening, but the sunless, clouded sky made it feel much later. All of the lamps had been lit earlier than usual and the air smelled of oncoming rain. He had tucked the mask under his cloak and wanted nothing more than to put it on and head straight into the library, but one by one he could see the lights dimming within and he knew he wouldn't have much time.

"Tomorrow," he whispered to himself.

The streets were relatively silent, or he might not have heard the footsteps in the distance behind him. He walked a little closer to one of the buildings until he could see the reflection of a woman in green behind him, just far enough so that she could disappear in the event that he suddenly turned around unexpectedly. He had finally spotted her, but as he was reveling in this accomplishment, an idea struck him that was so pleasing that he couldn't stop the smile that seemed to stretch across his entire face.

He looked around and then walked nonchalantly into a bakery. He knew this bakery well, for this was where he and Maribel often purchased treats for their evening excursions. He walked to a place just far enough away from the main counter so that no one would see him and yet was also blocked from the window by a tall shelf loaded with bread, freshly baked each morning.

Looking around to make sure no one was

watching, he quickly slipped the mask from his cloak. A nearby candle reflected the purple glow on its surface. He put it up to his face and, as Plumstone had instructed, cleared his mind and imagined who he wanted to be.

Before he could even wonder if it had worked, he realized that he was no longer holding on to anything but his chin, and when he opened his eyes, he saw that he was at least two feet taller than he had been a moment ago. It took all his willpower not to burst out laughing, which would have caused quite the scene.

He pulled off his crimson cloak and put back on his cap and then headed for the door. Standing on the opposite side of the street, just out of the street lamp's glow, was Amelia, and when Ben realized that she wasn't even paying attention to him, he decided to have a little more fun.

As he approached her, she was still staring

intently at the bakery door, waiting for a goblin to emerge any minute. He stopped alongside her and in a deeper voice than he usually used, he asked, "Excuse me, ma'am, do you have the time?"

She turned and looked straight at him and for a moment, he thought that perhaps she recognized him and that his ruse was over before it even had a chance to begin. Then she looked down and pulled out a pocket watch from under her green cloak.

"Nearly seven," she said tersely and then returned her focus to the door across the street.

"Thanks," he said, tipping his cap.

He wanted to run and shout and dance and sing with absolute joy. Instead he contented himself to walk up and down every street he could, relishing the simple fact that no one seemed to mind he was there. There were no harsh looks, no inquiring eyes, no mothers clutching their children tighter as he passed, no unspoken accusations. And for the first time in his life, he felt truly free.

Just when he thought the moment couldn't possibly get any better, he saw a woman walking toward him who he instantly recognized. He let her pass before pulling up alongside her.

"Have a good week?" he asked in his normal voice.

Maribel turned quickly but her face changed even quicker from happiness to confusion when she saw that the voice she knew too well wasn't coming from a goblin. "I'm sorry, do I know you?" she asked.

Ben tilted his head as though considering the question. "Yes and no," he said.

Maribel sighed, obviously irritated. "What kind of an answer is that?"

Ben shrugged. "The best I could think up."

Maribel shook her head, plunged her hands deeper into her pockets, and quickened her stride. "I don't have time for this. It's going to rain soon, and I have somewhere to be."

"Yeah, I think so, too. It's a good thing you bought me this hat for Christmas."

Maribel stopped so abruptly that Ben practically walked right into her.

She looked at him, really looked at him, this time. "It's you," she said, "but how?"

He couldn't stop the laugh from coming this time and when it had subsided, he took a deep breath and let it out slowly, relishing the moment.

"It's been an interesting week to say the least, I'll tell you about it on the way home."

16.
SUSPICION

Killan walked the countryside around Jotunfell as he had every night since December 23 of the prior year. He couldn't say why he did it. All he knew was that something had felt wrong; wrong from the moment he had left his brother and those humans to the mercy of his father.

At first, he contented himself to take a quick jaunt around the city walls, but over time, he extended his range to the surrounding woods, covering different areas each night. Tonight, as he had for the past week, he had felt the need to walk along the river's edge. His eyes darted to and fro, surveying all that laid before him. He wasn't sure why he looked so intently or what he was looking for, if anything.

On this night, though, many questions were suddenly answered, and many more presented themselves to be asked. Nearly half a mile from the city walls, he spotted something not natural stuck between a fallen branch and a rock. The rushing water was trying its best to take the object along with it and carry it downstream as far as the ocean but the chance falling of a tree only a day before impeded its progress.

It's interesting to think how something so small can have ramifications so far reaching. For example, if that tree had waited just ten more seconds to fall or had fallen at a slightly different angle, it would have never caught the objects as they passed by and our story would have a much different ending.

Killan approached the objects and knew

what they were before he even picked them up. Sodden, torn, and discolored though they were, they were unmistakably goblin wings.

"Three pairs," he whispered.

He felt the fabric between his fingers and then looked around. All that he could see from that vantage point were trees and more trees. And then, a light flickered to life in the distance, high above the forest, and Killan watched as the distant silhouette of his father passed in front of that light and looked out the window of his tower onto the darkening lands below.

AUTHOR'S NOTE

I've written a lot of stories in my life, but this is my first sequel. It's an entirely new experience, writing the further adventures of characters that you've already established, and I've really enjoyed visiting with them again.

As before, thanks are definitely in order for my wife Ashleigh, my friend Andrea, and my editor Parisa for all of your help in bringing out the best in this story.

Also, a special thanks to everyone who has supported my writing either by purchasing *The Good Goblin* and/or leaving me a review online. It has meant so much to me!

About the Author

David McElroy is a writer and designer who has been creating stories in one way or another since childhood. A chance pickup at an elementary school book fair began his fascination with goblins, and he's always believed they could be more than simple fodder for stalwart adventurers.

He lives in Lebanon, IL with his wife and daughter.

For more information, visit his website at www.davidmcelroybooks.com.